By Vilhelm Moberg

A TIME ON EARTH—translated from the Swedish
Din Stund på Jorden (*Thy Time on Earth*)

THE EMIGRANTS—translated from the Swedish
Utvandrarna (*The Emigrants*)

UNTO A GOOD LAND—translated from the Swedish
Invandrarna (*The Immigrants*)

THE LAST LETTER HOME—translated from the
Swedish
Nybyggarna (*The Settlers*) and *Sista brevet till
Sverige* (*The Last Letter to Sweden*)

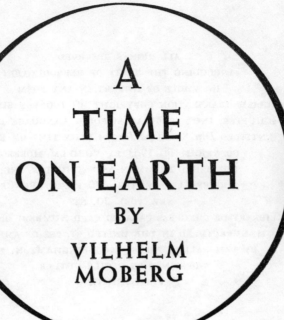

A
TIME
ON EARTH
BY
VILHELM
MOBERG

Translated from the Swedish by
NAOMI WALFORD

SIMON AND SCHUSTER
NEW YORK

A TIME ON EARTH

THE PLACE WHERE I live is on the shore of the Pacific. The greatest of the world's oceans surges just outside, and Room 20, the Pacific Hotel, Surf Street, Pine Beach, is my home on earth.

My room has two windows. Through the one facing the street, I see automobiles and trucks moving in an endless stream; through the other I watch the arching rollers of the ocean. The roar of traffic and the rushing of the surf—the noises from the street to the east and the water to the west—blend in my ears. The cars on Surf Street sound like the whirring of a giant spinning wheel, unceasing, while the thunder of the sea rises and falls with the movement of the waves, like breathing from the depths of the world's lung. The engines roar, crash and rattle; the waves of the deep smash themselves against the rocks of the shore with the sound of great guns, so that the water shoots upward and washes the tops of the cypresses. In daytime the voice of the town prevails, at night that of the sea. By day the noise of engines holds sway over my ears; at night the ocean rules alone.

The sound of the street is as young as the street itself, the sound of the sea as old as the elements. The motor voice will fall silent and the spinning wheel stop, while the ocean continues to hurl its breakers to the

7

beach. Then the sea will be the sovereign ruler by day and by night.

I live between the man-made and a primal element, being myself an incidental phenomenon on the earth. Between the ephemeral and the eternal I have my home.

In this incidental existence I am one of the inhabitants of the little town of Pine Beach in Southern California, one immigrant among the mass of immigrants from Europe. Here the weather is pleasantly mild, the sun pleasantly hot, the wind pleasantly cool, the sea water pleasantly warm. Orange trees grow, and fine fruits ripen. This is the last settler-state, the last frontier. An average of 1,700 people arrive here on each of the 365 days of the year. The daily throng of newcomers is large enough to form a community of its own; a new town could be founded here every day. Young people come to our coast in search of the ancient, original sources of joy—sun and sea—and here they start a new life.

Here, for the young, life feels young. For me, Albert Carlson, an old immigrant, it is otherwise. I am of an age when the power of renewal is lost. The days have now come when I no longer experience anything that seems to me worth experiencing.

At one stage in my life I had a series of places to live in. I lived in houses, equipped and furnished with all the mechanical gadgets that man has invented for his greater convenience and comfort. I had spacious houses to live in, but I never felt at home in any of them. I did not stay long in any of them. I had several dwellings, but no home.

Here in my hotel room with the number 20 on the door I shall stay as long as I can. I wrote recently to my elder son, who was christened Albert after me: "I intend to stay here in Pine Beach and live in a hotel for the rest of my life, if I can afford it. I shall sit here at my window, looking out over the Pacific and thinking about some of the things I've done and known."

From now on I want to be stationary. The later years of my life have been largely spent in traveling. The object of a journey is to arrive at a certain geographical point; yet for my journeys there was no goal anywhere on the globe. Judged by results they were futile: they had no results. I sought something that I was forced to seek, but the goal was within the traveler himself and not to be found elsewhere: I was looking for protection against my awareness. That is what kept me on the move, pursued me and forced me to fresh departures. Journeys for me were like narcotics against pain: they relieved the symptoms but never touched the cause.

How many times in my life have I moved from place to place! But for me physical removal solves nothing.

So I am still in flight, and the pursuer is a knowledge which I wrestle with—an insight I cannot bear. It visits me by day; it comes to me at night. In the evenings before I fall asleep it lingers by me, and it is present in the morning when I wake. It is the realization that my life is over. The life that was worth living is over for me. And from that realization one question inevitably arises: How did I use that life?

In the end I've become a solitary man in a hotel room. I might have gone on traveling if my financial situation hadn't changed; now I can no longer afford it. But I feel more at home here in my room at the Pacific than in the big, comfortable houses I once lived in. The smaller my dwelling, the better do I know every inch of its space; the increase of square yards brings increase in loneliness.

In my present existence I feel as if life's gift were used up; what remains seems to me unimportant. The days, months or years that lie ahead can change nothing, restore no lost opportunities, never help me to attain anything I might still desire.

I see myself now as living on the narrowest possible strip of land, having been washed up there from a boundless ocean; here by effort and exertion I cling fast, awaiting the only thing that can still happen to me: waiting for the same seas that carried me here to take me back again—wash me away from my little foothold and in their depths bestow upon me the sleep that has no end.

At night when this awareness forces itself upon me, I lie and listen to the motion of the Pacific on the beach below the hotel terrace. I flee from my pursuer into things heard. In my ears I follow the rhythm of the breakers as they hurl themselves against the granite bastions of the rocks and are smashed upon them. I listen to the ocean's cannonade against the fortress shore. The wave recedes but another comes on. The sea reloads its gun, fires its rumbling shot, and again a wave smashes itself against the rocks in a cascade of water, as of a cloudburst. I hear the fall of huge and heavy raindrops.

The crash and murmur from the shore fill my ears, but they cannot drive away my persecutor. The questions of my thoughts are posed again, and repeated. Yet there is no answer to them—they merely dash themselves to pieces against a granite wall. They are hurled back, washed away. But they return again, ever again, like the rollers from the waste of waters.

There it is again: the knowledge that my life is past. What have I left? What remains for me? I find only one answer: to resign myself and await the wave that will carry me back whence I came.

Surf Street, my street, is the main street of Pine Beach and also the highway that runs north and south along the California coast. Buildings sprang up beside this road and clustered into a town; within a few years the population doubled. Smoke from the oil wells pollutes the air of the great city of Los Angeles, but here in little Pine Beach the sea winds keep the air clean and fresh for us. We are also spared the fierce heat that prevails farther inland, beyond the mountains.

We have had no rain here since the beginning of April this year, 1962, and we are now at the end of July. We shall have none before November. From my east window I can see the high hills, where green growth has been scorched by the sun. The grasses stand dry and withered and rustle bleakly in the gusty wind. The slopes are reddish brown and I sometimes fancy that they smell burned, like a roast forgotten in the oven. Only the thorny clumps of giant cactus, the one plant of the necessary stamina, show up in splashes of green.

Singed by the sun, the hills raise their backs like vast, petrified, prehistoric dinosaurs watching over the town below them.

Pine Beach is well situated between sea and hills. The ocean cools the air we breathe; the mountains shelter us from the desert winds. The sea is in eternal motion, the mountains in eternal repose.

I have just returned from a journey to the place where I was born. Only a week ago I was at the other side of the world. A week ago I was sitting in another hotel room. This hotel was in an industrial community in Småland, Sweden, and the room was much like my present one in the Pacific Hotel, Pine Beach: it was entirely modern, and fitted out on the American pattern. Motor traffic rolled along the street outside, though more sparsely, and the makes of the vehicles were in most cases the same as on Surf Street. Next to the hotel, as here, was a filling station where brands of oil were advertised in English. In the center of the town was a bar where ice cream, Coca-Cola and hamburgers were served, and where there was also a jukebox which emitted a ceaseless stream of songs and dance music: hits from America. Above the counter hung a sign: DRIVE-IN BAR. Posters announced that the "Sweden Artists" were appearing in a Jack Dalley Show in the Folk Park, and that the Andersons' enormously popular twist band, "New Sound Twist Pop," provided the dance music.

America had overtaken me and was moving into my old home district. Each time I have been back to my country I have noticed the changes: each time, Sweden has become less Swedish.

Now, by the roads of the air, I had made another journey home, but not to stay. Not for a moment did I imagine that a final return to Sweden was possible for the old emigrant who bore my name. The Swedish-Americans of my age who go back to find the home of their childhood are the victims of self-deception. There can be no return to that country for anyone. I can go

13

back in the superficial sense, to the soil, the houses, trees, waters, fields. I can go back to things, but never to the domain of childhood. There can be no retracing of one's steps to the world of growing up, for this world has turned into dreams and memories forever. Here I stand rebuffed outside a door that is barred.

After more than forty years in the United States I have become a foreigner in the land where I was born and bred. Father and Mother are dead, my brothers and sisters are dead. Some of my relatives survive, and some contemporaries I knew in my childhood, but among them I am almost entirely forgotten. I am just a name to be mentioned with the added comment: "He went to America."

This was to be my last visit to Sweden. Why did I go? I wanted to see the countryside of my childhood in summer. I wanted to lay a wreath on my parents' grave. Once again I wanted to visit the parish church-yard where Father, Mother, sisters and brothers have been made one with the soil. Once again I wanted to see the place where many generations of my family have returned to dust. Their youth, maturity, wandering through the world and vanishing into the earth— this perpetual cycle I behold most clearly in the grave-yard of my home parish.

I know Swedish-Americans who have moved back to Sweden in their old age because they wanted to be buried among their forefathers and reunited with them: a child's return to the womb. I can understand these returned wanderers and feel with them, but I remain unmoved by the blood-and-family mystique. What do I care about the exact spot where the earth is to take back my dead body? That body will no longer

14

be myself, and what happens to it can in no way concern me.

Yet the parish churchyard is the one place in my native village where almost all the people belonging to the world that once was mine are gathered. There, with that world, they have vanished.

One evening at the beginning of June I stepped off the train at my childhood's station. One evening in May forty-two years ago I had boarded the train at that same station, in the direction from which I now came: that was Emigration Day. I remembered, and reflected, It is between those two evenings that my real life has passed.

I put down my suitcase on the platform. And for a minute or two after alighting I stood motionless as if in ritual observance of the day, forty-two years earlier, on which I had boarded a train from that same station. On that day I was not alone; my sister Jenny saw me off (Father and Mother refused to come). And I said goodbye to several people on the platform. That evening I was the most notable person on the express.

Now I stood here alone. No one had come to meet me. No one knew that I was arriving. Quite a crowd had gathered at the station, but I saw not a soul whom I recognized or who recognized me.

I glanced back at my train, now disappearing round the bend where there had once been a watchman's hut. For the last hour of my train journey I had been the sole passenger in the compartment. The guard told me that the railway would probably be closed down now that buses had taken over passenger traffic. In 1872 the isolated world of this district had been opened up by the steel rails. For ninety years train wheels had rolled over the steel miles. My mother used to tell us that when she was six years old she was at the inauguration of the railway, and saw the king; this was a tremendous event, for it was the only time in all her life that she ever set eyes on a king.

Every Sunday we boys went to the station to look at the train, which halted there barely one minute. We looked chiefly at the engine, coughing out its steam in a way that sounded like a giant's laughter. Now after ninety years' service the wheels will come to a halt and the engine will wind up in a railway museum, where the youth of a new day will laugh at the funny old contraption.

I looked down the line in the opposite direction, where there was a long, straight stretch. Many steel miles lie there under sentence of death. Soon the rumble of the train will cease, the forest will take back its own, and quietness will rule over the deserted roadbed. And in time to come people will say, "There was a railway here once. You can still see the track."

Those who had gathered on the platform to meet the train had now dispersed, and I stood alone there with my suitcase like a lost foreigner. A kindly railwayman spoke to me as he came past: "There's a cab stand just behind the station, if you want a taxi." I thanked him, but remarked that the new Station Hotel was quite close, and I could make it on foot. The railwayman looked astonished: How could *I* know about the new Station Hotel?

I was aware that a large community had grown up round the station during my absence: new streets, new

16

houses, shops, filling stations, buses crammed with passengers. Earlier visits had shown me that my home village had fundamentally altered.

I now found that great changes had taken place even since my last visit. I was staggered by all the innovations from abroad, mainly from the United States. But things adopted from America and transplanted here clashed with the surroundings; they looked unnatural. I could never have imagined them in the setting of my Småland home. I was accustomed to them in another country, but in this one they seemed foreign.

I strayed vaguely about my home parish. I recognized no one I met along the roads, and nobody knew me. I met a few of my contemporaries of childhood days, but only with an effort could I find them in their aged and altered faces; these were not the people I had known. And they found it as difficult to find me, in my face: they knew who I was, but doubted what they knew. We were strangers. To the families that had sprung up since I left the neighborhood I seemed a specter—the wraith of one departed who had come back to life and was trying to force his way into the house where he had once lived.

I was back, but irrevocably shut out. I felt like a tourist in my own country. I now had the final confirmation: I no longer belonged here, for the place to which I had belonged had ceased to exist.

Walking about among those unknown people in that alien countryside, I remembered a legend that my grandmother had told me. It made such a strong impression on me that more than once I asked her to repeat it.

Once upon a time there were two friends who exchanged a sacred vow: Each would attend the other's wedding, wherever he might be at the time. One of them died, and some time afterward the other was to be married. He grieved that his dearest friend would not be present. But late at night the dead man came to the bridal house. He sat down behind the front door and would take no refreshment but a handful of earth and a mug of water. But when the bridal dance was played, the dead man honored his living friend's bride and danced with her three times. Later as he was about to go on his way, he said to the bridegroom, "Now you must keep your promise to me! I too am celebrating my wedding tonight, and you must come with me." The bridegroom would rather have stayed with his young bride, but could not break his promise to his friend, and so he went with him.

The friends came to a house where many people had gathered in a large, brightly lit room. They entered, and the dead man said to his friend, "I danced three times with your bride; now you shall dance three times with mine."

And the living man danced three times with the dead man's bride. Then he returned to his own house.

He had been away only a short time, but when he came back everything about the place had changed. The house where he had left his bride was gone, and in its place stood a new building inhabited by people unknown to him. He went to other homes, but of the people he saw and met he knew not one, and no one knew him. Then he went to the parish priest who had so recently married him and his bride. But the priest too was a stranger. The man told him who he was and the name of his town, and explained that he had left his own wedding celebration the evening before and gone with a deceased friend to his wedding in the realm of the dead. But now he could find neither his bride nor his house.

The priest opened the old church register and found that all the man said was true. His name was in the books, but it was the name of a dead parishioner. The register showed that he had lived in the parish, and had celebrated his wedding there three hundred years before.

One hundred years had passed for each dance he had danced at his dead friend's wedding. And when he heard this there was nothing for him to do but to return to the realm of death.

Now I felt just like that ghost in the legend, who could not find his bride or his home. I was an unknown person in an unknown place which was inhabited by unknown people. I had been absent for a shorter period than the man in the legend, for only forty years had elapsed since I lived in that parish; but it might just as well have been three hundred years. It would have made no difference, for I could not have felt more of a stranger. I had emerged from the past and was haunting my home.

Like the other ghost, I could have gone to the parish priest. If he had opened his registers he would have found me, and learned that I was born in his parish of Sjöhult sixty-four years ago. He would have seen that I was the son of Ernst Gottfrid Karlsson, a crofter, and his wife Anna Magdalena Johansdotter, who lived in the laborer's croft called Lindkullen, of Högaberg village, and later owned a sixteenth of a *mantal*, freehold, in Källebäck village. He would also have seen that in May, 1920, I took out immigration papers for the United States and that today I am the only one left of the Karlssons' eight children.

I am the sole survivor of that flock born in the Lindkullen croft: one room and kitchen. But I did not look for that cabin, which was gone before I myself left; I sought no bridal house or bride. I had come to visit the dead.

I stayed six weeks in Sweden: the same length of time as in 1949, when my father died. My mother's death had occurred five years earlier, during the Second World War, so I had not been able to go to her funeral.

This time I spent the whole six weeks in my home district. Most of the day I walked about the fields and meadows, imagining that I might still come upon the places where I could rediscover myself as a barefoot youngster. But even the fields were changed. I looked for glades and clearings where I had gorged myself on wild strawberries and whortleberries, for bogs and marshes where I had plucked the bitter cranberries. But clearings and glades were overgrown with dense woodland; marshes and bogs had been drained now and yielded oats instead of cranberries. What had once been woodland was now bare, and vice versa; I recognized nothing. I wandered at random, lost in my native countryside.

But on one of my wanderings I came to a patch of juniper which had been part of our homestead in Källebäck village. It lay in a little enclosure where we grazed our sheep; we called it the sheep paddock. Here the dry, bare old juniper bushes still stood. The juniper patch of my childhood was as it had always been, and here I found my young self again.

I love the juniper and its fruit, those bitter, hard berries; a beer is brewed from them that brings a tang of the woods to the tongue. The juniper beer that my mother brewed was the good drink of my childhood. I love the juniper bush, that tough, unnecessary growth that is thinned out to make room for useful trees; that enduring, hardy bush that can never be eradicated; juniper the disliked, that never flatters or ingratiates, and cannot be shaped or trimmed, but grows as it will; the bush with the spiny twigs, the weed of the woods. It may be cut down, burned, dragged out by the roots, yet it grows again; it comes back. At last it reaches the very doorstep, but not until the house has become a house of mourning. When someone within is dead, it is the old custom to set the finest juniper bushes to stand guard before the house, one on each side of the steps. Then at last the weed of the woods comes into its own, with honor.

Here in our old sheep paddock this eccentric of the countryside remained as it had been in my childhood. We met again. I put both my arms round the biggest bush, and it responded by pricking my hands. It scratched me with its sharp twig-claws till my skin smarted. It tore and stabbed my hands. It was a painful embrace, and I felt the sting of it long afterward, but at the moment I felt that I had come back. I was home again.

There among the junipers it was a meeting and a farewell. Never again shall I see the place where I was born.

After six weeks as a ghost in my old mother country, I came back to the land where I shall die.

✟✟✟✟

HERE IN MY HOTEL ROOM between town and ocean my
days pass without event. The society of my two neighbors fills my life: the town exhausts me, the sea re-
stores my strength. In the mornings I go straight from
my bed to the beach and let the waves hurl themselves
over my body. They drench it, wash away the drowsi-
ness left by the sleep and stupor of the night. In the
evenings I make the same journey and drown the accumulated tiredness of the day. The ocean is reviving
to my spirits. Doctors have told me that this is due to
the presence of potassium in the water. The same salt
is used in tablets prescribed for mental weariness and
strain. But whatever may or may not be the influence
of potassium on a man's soul, it is very certain that my
vital forces are renewed in the Pacific: It is my Great
Helper.

Yet the sea that gives me life has also tried to take it
from me. Once the attempt nearly succeeded. I turned
my back on my Helper a few seconds too long. I had
not yet learned to follow the motion of the waves and
did not know the danger of turning one's back on the
ocean. I was attacked from behind by a mighty breaker
that swept me to the shore and flung me against a rock.
Shocked, battered and dizzy, I fell into a cleft. I was
half fainting, but managed to cling fast to my cleft as
the wave was dragging me back, so that it receded

alone. If on the threshold of unconsciousness I had been swept out again, it would have been the end of me. As it was, I escaped with aches and pains. I hit my knee on a sharp edge of rock, and was lame for a couple of months afterward.

The sea had dealt me a mighty blow which nearly tossed me to the place where no time is.

Since then I have learned the enormous power and pace of my Helper. A wave several times my own height may rise up before me at any moment, knock me senseless and helpless, and carry me out on its foaming crest like a blade of grass from the shore.

At any second of my contact with the world's largest ocean, its waters may drag me from my incidental little strip of land and wash me away.

Nine-tenths of my reading consists of history, and at present I am looking for books about my dangerous neighbor and Great Helper. My knowledge of the subject is still elementary. The known history of the Pacific is short, and goes back no farther than the year 1520, when it was named by the man who first sailed upon it. Magellan voyaged over these unknown waters during a long period of calm, and because of this he called them *Il Pacifico*.

To one living as its neighbor 450 years later it still seems a calm, placid sea in relation to its size. "A sea so vast that the human mind can scarcely grasp it," writes Maximilian Transylvanus in his account. For millions of years it was untraveled and nameless; only during the last few brief centuries has it been known to men as the Pacific Ocean. I can learn no more than a minute fraction of its history.

At night, when I have lain long awake and turned and turned in my bed, I get up, dress and go out. I go down to the shores of the Pacific, and walk over the sand dunes to the north, beyond the town. When the sky brightens above the sea I turn back, and as I retrace my steps the ocean discards the night mist, which disperses and drifts away over the mountains to the east. Low tide, and the beach is at its widest. The waters have withdrawn and for a time have lent a part of their domain to the land. At low tide I pace the floor of the sea, a solitary walker over the dunes at dawn.

Near these great waters my unease is stilled. Ocean winds lay their gentle, soothing hands upon my tired, burning eyelids. I breathe calmly. My nostrils draw in the scent of plants from the deep: grasses, seaweed, the coils of giant kelp—all the fragrances and salts of the water. And through skin, nose and mouth I am revived.

I think of the man who discovered this ocean and gave it the name of Pacific. Day after day, week after week, for more than a hundred days, Magellan sailed this sea. His vessels were the first the ocean ever bore. He sailed over a surface as empty and deserted as was the earth itself on the first morning of Creation.

Men lived in the world for a hundred thousand years without knowing of an ocean that occupied more than a third of the earth's surface.

My other neighbor rumbles below my east window. The town makes itself heard most insistently at the end of the working day, in the rush hour. I stand now looking out over Main Street, Pine Beach, where the lines of automobiles grow denser and crawl ever more slowly. Every shop sign in the street is well known to me, and I recognize people moving along the sidewalk. I have lived here so long now that I know the faces of many Pine Beach folk. Sometimes I stop in the street and talk to passersby whose names I don't know.

In the building nearest to my hotel Mrs. Jeffers runs her real-estate office. Every time I see her signboard I am reminded of my own career as a real-estate agent. How many of my adult years—the best in life—did I spend in real-estate offices? I don't want to count; there were too many. Now I cannot understand how I lived through them. Business was never enough to fill my life; it always left a void within me. And when I look back at this emptiness I wonder whether for all those years I was abusing the gift of life.

I have a bond with Mrs. Jeffers. But she has run her business so successfully that it has become the largest of its kind in this little town. She has an office staff of five, all women. In this country one often finds women in the real-estate business; they seem well qualified to buy, sell and let houses. Mrs. Jeffers, a plump, middle-aged, energetic and talkative lady, often stops me in the street to confide her professional worries to me. She knows of my earlier life and regards me as a colleague, an authority on the house business. She speaks continuously of her husband, who is continually away. If I am to believe her, he is an excellent man in all respects, but for some inexplicable reason he is never with her. I have never seen him and doubt that he is to be found in this world.

Opposite the Pacific Hotel is the fish restaurant, Lobster House. Mr. Collins, the proprietor, stands in the doorway as if looking for customers among the passersby. He is an Irishman with a German wife. I have often heard them quarreling, and I imagine that even at this moment Mrs. Collins is bawling someone out in the kitchen. The lobster at Lobster House is excellent, but the proprietor sometimes appears in the dining room drunk. This annoys the customers, who feel that he is usurping their prerogative. The restaurant is not doing well, either because of Mr. Collins' weakness for strong drink or because of the Pine Beach inhabitants' indifference to fish. It is Mrs. Collins, the efficient German, who keeps the place going.

A little farther down Surf Street the Irishman has a formidable competitor in the Mexican Juan Rodríguez Cabrillo's little eating house, which bears the sign MEXICAN FOOD. BREAKFAST SERVED ALL ROUND THE CLOCK. Rodríguez Cabrillo is the name of the discoverer of California, and the restaurant proprietor avers that he is this hero's direct descendant. When I go to Cabrillo's I avoid his Mexican dishes, which are too highly spiced for my palate. But he grills meat very well and serves a good draught beer. Today MEXICAN FOOD is dark; it is Monday, and Cabrillo closes on Mondays.

Near the intersection of San Pedro Street is my drugstore, where morning and afternoon I buy my paper. Every time I go in I have a little conversation with Mrs. Boles, the proprietor. She is a very talkative woman, but she often hits the nail on the head. She is well read; she reads philosophical works. Bertrand Russell is her favorite author. I am surprised that she runs a drugstore, even though it is her own, and feel that she might have held quite a different position in life.

Today the front page of the evening edition of the Los Angeles *Times* carried prominent headlines about new nuclear bomb tests in both East and West. The hydrogen bomb that had been set off was one of the most powerful to date, and stocks of such bombs were piling up in both hemispheres. Mrs. Boles handed me the paper, asking what I thought of human beings who went on acquiring and stocking nuclear weapons. They had already collected enough to destroy us. Now they were behaving like some would-be suicide who already has an effective weapon to kill himself with but goes on buying more and more revolvers and stacking them in a heap, just to be on the safe side.

I answered, "It's just to be on the safe side that people are stockpiling the means of our destruction."

Mrs. Boles went on to observe that Bertrand Russell once said or wrote that the human race would probably be wiped out before the year 2000, so at most we had thirty-eight years left to us on earth.

"What do you think about that, Mr. Carlson?"

I replied that I had no particular views on the question, but that from what I had read of the period during which man had inhabited the earth, he seemed to me to be the most tenacious of all animals. In the course of his existence he had endured untold evil and been afflicted by unimaginable disasters; yet he had survived and multiplied to a point where the earth could no longer feed its population. And so I supposed that some proportion of humanity would survive nuclear warfare as well.

I am standing at my window now, looking out for a man whom I usually see at the San Pedro intersection, not far from the drugstore, at this time of day. And he is there now. He is a head taller than the passersby on the sidewalk, and is also distinguished from them by his dress. He wears a green ankle-length overcoat, and his thick, bushy brown hair falls to his shoulders. He has a long, unkempt beard of a darker color that covers his chest.

This man always stands at the Surf-San Pedro crossing during the rush hour, when the lines of cars are densest. One might think he was working as an official traffic checker. But he is there on his own most private business and mission: his aim is to abolish automobiles from the face of the earth. He is the town idiot who stands at his post in the thick of the traffic for one hour daily. Every time a vehicle halts at the crossing, he shouts to the driver, "Stop driving! Stop driving!" In other states he would no doubt have been arrested for obstructing the traffic or for disorderly conduct, but in our little California settler-town an eccentric may still walk freely about the streets. The man is regarded as harmless; everybody knows him, and nobody now pays any attention to his behavior.

The man with the gownlike coat and the wild hair and beard is Jensen: an immigrant from Denmark. To Americans who fail to distinguish between the Nordic countries he is a Scandinavian and thus my compatriot. Outwardly he resembles the Christ figure as represented in paintings, and the people of Pine Beach have christened him Jesus Jensen.

I always exchange a few words with Jesus Jensen when I meet him in the street. He talks calmly and collectedly, and seems a perfectly ordinary, normal person. There is nothing of the preacher or prophet about him—nothing theatrical or ecstatic—nothing unusual beyond his attitude toward motorists. At times I have wanted to ask him why he exhorts them to abolish their cars. But how can one ask a person why he's mad?

During the great rush hour the ocean's voice is

drowned by the noise of the street. But the rumble, rattle and clatter of the town is pierced suddenly by a treble note, a silvery chime, the ringing of a bell. This is the gentle sound of the twilight hour: the ice-cream boy announcing his arrival.

At this signal women and children come out of the houses and surround the little truck with the ringing bell. They've been waiting for it; they flock and jostle round it. The van of glory is enameled white, and the ice-cream boy is dressed to match, in white from head to foot. On his head he wears a pointed cap—a goblin's cap. He is the goblin of the fairy tales, bringing children his luscious vanilla ices, and they shout and jostle and scream as they shove forward. The silver chime of the bell and the high childish voices mingle with the deafening roar of the traffic. The ice-cream boy with his white truck is the children's delight, that appears on Surf Street, Pine Beach, every day at dusk.

Darkness falls swiftly over the street, and the signs light up. Mrs. Jeffers closes her real-estate office for the day. Collins goes into the dining room of the Lobster House to await his dinner guests; the ice-cream seller's truck drives down the street and disappears as the silvery chime dies away. But the tall figure in the coat like a mantle remains in his place at the intersection, and the breeze sweeps in gusts over his long beard. Like a rock he stands in the ocean of traffic, shouting, "Stop driving!" The cars drive on and the man's voice is drowned in the roar of motors. Jesus Jensen stands at his post till the end of his watch.

The town vanishes in the dusk. I move over to the west window of my hotel room; from here I can survey my other neighbor. Toward evening the rollers subside. It is almost low tide, and the sea darkens under the arch of the sky. Catalina Island, which rises in the west like a rocky fortress, has vanished. The blue-black expanse of ocean is edged by white surf. The sea's voice drops to a gentler note, a peaceful murmur. The lung of the world breathes more softly toward night.

I dwell between the town and the ocean, and tonight I shall again fall asleep with the sound of the sea lingering in my ears.

BUT WHEN I LIE AWAKE AT NIGHT I sometimes hear
the sound of other waters—waters far away. It is a distant stream running in a narrow, winding channel
through woods and the meadows in another country. Its
murmur is softer and gentler than the sea's. No great
breakers come crashing in. It is a brook that mingles its
pure and limpid note with the roar of the hugest ocean
in the world: the stream of my childhood, where a
week or two back I met my brother.

Something I cannot explain happened to me during
my last visit home. It had to do with Sigfrid, my elder
brother. We met again after fifty years. We were torn
apart in 1912, and since then half a century has passed.
We found each other once more in 1962, and the meeting occurred as I was wandering among the fields of
home. Sigfrid came back to me, or I to him.

This was not in my dreams at night, but while I was
awake in bright daylight. How it happened I will not
attempt to explain. I know I can't; nor do I believe
that anyone else could—no more than anyone could
explain to me what life is, or death, so as to convince
me. No one can tell me what the purpose of my life is,
if indeed it has any, and no one can tell me what death
will do to me at the moment life ends. Many believe
that I shall just be tipped into extinction—that death is
nothingness. But while I am still alive I cannot con-

ceive of nothingness, so I am none the wiser. I am and must remain ignorant of what I most of all desire to know.

As little do I understand how it came about that my brother Sigfrid and I were reunited in our home district, after fifty years.

It was during my last evening there. I was walking along the stream called Bjurbäck, which got its name in the times long past when the beaver still built his dams across it. In my boyhood it flowed swiftly, and flooded the meadows in spring and autumn. It was rich in fish. Now I found the water meadows drained and tilled and transformed into fields of oats, and the stream dug out and nearly dry. The channel lay bare, showing ugly slabs of rock; it wound along like a stone serpent. Here Sigfrid and I used to catch a great many fish: pike and burbot. But in the small pools of stagnant, stale water that lingered between the stones after the digging out of the stream no fish remained. I saw not a fin move. The shimmering film known to us as "blue-silver" covered the surface, proving that there was no life beneath. Blue-silver lies on water like a lid on a coffin: the lid of death lay on my childhood's stream.

Walking beside the Bjurbäck, I came to a glade in the fir wood where the watercourse made a sharp bend. It was then it happened.

I stopped and remained standing there; I recognized the place, I remembered, I was overwhelmed with memory. I heard and saw. I was back again. I was standing here at this moment—but also at another moment long, long ago. Then and now mingled and became only Now.

I was standing at a place where Sigfrid and I used to rest during our fishing. Just here, on the ground under

32

my feet, we would make a fire and roast pike on the embers; here we ate what we had brought with us; here we stretched out on our backs and relaxed. And here we once lay looking up at the clouds and my brother Sigfrid said, "I'm only on earth this time—this one time! I must take good care of my life!"

Other words of his have rung in my head for fifty years; they were the last he spoke to me before we parted: "Shall we go to the brook on Sunday?" When he had said that, he left me.

And now we met again. This was the place, the spot where I was standing. I recognized it, and looked in the grass for charred wood and ashes from our campfire. Something must be left. . . . And I seemed to see traces of the fire that had burned here fifty years ago, lit by two boys.

Here at our old resting place my brother and I met again. He came toward me; I recognized his voice; I could not mistake it—it could not be confused with anyone else's. Afterward I wondered whether I had caught the echo of it—whether the echo of a voice could linger in a place and be heard fifty years later.

Sigfrid met me here, and he was in no way changed. But I who had come back was different. My brother was young, I was old.

Sigfrid said, "You've come back. You've been away a long time. I'm here still. I know you still remember me. And I'm the same. Nothing has happened to me. You remember me well. You remember . . . we were often together, you and I."

Thus it was that my brother Sigfrid came back. Since then he has never left me.

And again I live through the hour when last we spoke together—the time we parted.

33

SIGFRID WAS MY ELDER BROTHER, and my only brother —the only one I ever knew. My other brothers had died in infancy, before I was born, and since I never shared a single day with them, I can hardly call them my brothers.

My brother was five years older than I, and I admired him for his strength and cleverness. Yet he treated me not as his junior but as an equal, so we had more in common than children of different ages usually have. We both worked on our father's farm and shared the cramped dwelling of our parents; we were what the Swedes call "home sons." For the first nine years of my life we lived in one room and kitchen: the crofter's cabin at Lindkullen. After that we slept in the same room in the little farmhouse on the sixteenth of a *mantal* which, after ceaseless toiling and saving, Father and Mother were able to buy. We lived as close to one another as people can live, he and I.

It happened in the summer of 1912. Sigfrid was then nineteen and I fourteen; we had lived on the farm for five years. It was a Sunday morning in July, in the larger of the two rooms. Here the whole family slept: Father, Mother, my three sisters, Sigfrid and I. It was early in the morning; Father, and Mother and I were up, but my sisters were still asleep.

On that Sunday morning Sigfrid stayed in his bed by

the farther long wall. He had not left it since the Friday before. On Friday evening he had gone to bed early, long before the rest of us. He just said he felt tired. He had said that on many evenings that summer, so I paid no particular attention. But after that he just lay there and slept; I never saw him open his eyes once, or heard him speak.

He had not been well that summer. The previous winter he had gone out into the world, and been away from home for some months. But in the spring when he came back he was not himself. All he said to me was that sometimes his back hurt and he felt tired. In the summer he had not brought his scythe to the mowing, though he had got up every morning as usual. I did not know what to make of his lying in bed in the daytime.

I asked Father and Mother why Sigfrid slept so long, and wouldn't he wake up soon, but received only vague answers. And I had no idea why my brother had been so different this summer; this I learned only afterward. I was regarded as a child, to be shielded from all that children don't understand and should not be concerned with. So I was worried: Sigfrid had gone to bed on Friday; now it was Sunday morning and he had not awakened.

When I saw Father and Mother standing by my brother's bed, I got up and stood beside them.

Sigfrid was breathing heavily and slowly in his sleep. His chin went up and down in an odd way as he breathed. I had never seen any sleeping person's chin move like that. Heavily and lingeringly it sank, then just as slowly and sluggishly it rose again. I watched this slow movement, and saw how the skin of his jaw wrinkled as it went down and smoothed out again when it went up.

I had many questions to ask my parents but was worried and afraid and could say nothing.

From my sisters' beds came the sound of light, calm breathing. But Father and Mother and I stood by my brother's bed, listening and watching. From a nail in the wall above his pillow hung his pocket watch, and the even ticking of the second hand sounded very clearly. On the wall above the watch was a picture, an oleograph in a broad black frame: JESUS HEALS THE SICK. There sat the barefoot Jesus in a red mantle by a rock on the shore of the Lake of Gennesaret. On the ground about him was a cluster of miserable, sick people, some with crutches under their arms, others open-mouthed as if crying out in pain. A paralyzed man lay on a bier by the bare feet of the Saviour. Jesus' feet gleamed so pure and white against the red mantle. Cripples and maimed people crawled around Jesus, stretching out their arms to him and crying out for life and health.

Sigfrid's eyes were tight shut, but his cheeks had begun to flush a little and his eyelids twitched slightly. Father said, "He looks as if he might be waking up," and Mother thought so too: "Yes, he's waking." I waited tensely for my brother to open his eyes at last. He had slept for so long that he *must* wake up.

But his chin moved more and more slowly, and what happened was not what we were waiting for, but something quite different: his chin stopped on the way up. It stopped and stayed still. It remained motionless while the wrinkles in the skin smoothed out. My brother's chin had stopped halfway, lacking strength to go any farther.

The sound of the heavy, slow breathing had ceased, and a new silence was in the room. From the other beds, where my sisters were sleeping and breathing calmly and evenly, the same sound continued. And the watch on the wall ticked on. A branch of the great chestnut at the end of the cottage brushed against the windowpane.

But one sound had gone, and everything was so quiet that I just had to say something to my parents; I had to know, I had to be told. But before I could open my mouth I was forestalled by Father.

He bent over my brother's face, straightened himself again and looked at the wall. Then he took down Sigfrid's watch from the nail and looked searchingly at the dial, as if to assure himself that the watch was still going.

Turning to us slowly with the watch in his hand, he said, "Twenty past seven. Exactly twenty past."

Father was telling us all of a sudden what time it was. Why? Nobody had asked him. And if we had wanted to know, we could have seen for ourselves.

Mother made no answer. Exactly twenty minutes past seven—but Mother said nothing. She just stood there, pressing a corner of her apron against her face. She had already been out and done the milking, and had spilled some milk on the apron. She brought with her a smell of cow; I was standing so close to her that I could smell the cow shed.

It was my job to drive the cows to pasture in the mornings. I ought to have done it by now, but I had stayed in because my brother hadn't waked up.

Sigfrid's watch, which Father was now holding in his hand, ticked so loudly in the new silence that the noise of it filled the room. It was called a lever watch, and was said to be a better timekeeper than the cylinder-escapement watch; it was attached to a shiny electroplated chain. In my childhood a large deep watch pocket was sewn into men's waistcoats, and the watch chain was supposed to be strung across the whole width of waistcoat and stomach, as an adornment to male dress.

In his bed Sigfrid lay stretched on his back, motionless. After his chin stopped I saw no other movement in him. Yet in Father's hand his watch ticked on. It seemed to be going faster than before, as if suddenly in a hurry.

Exactly twenty minutes past seven, Father said. Yet the second hand kept moving on round its track. By now it must be twenty-one or twenty-two minutes past. It went on as before. And I had got up as usual, and Mother had milked today as she always did, Sundays and weekdays. Yet this Sunday was not a morning like other mornings: Father had mentioned a time by the clock which we ought to remember.

My father turned to me, handed me Sigfrid's watch and said, "You shall have your brother's watch."

Silently and marveling, I took it. The plated watch chain twisted round my fingers. I still did not grasp what had happened.

Suddenly it was I who was holding Sigfrid's watch in my hand. The nail it had hung on stood out naked and empty. But immediately over my brother's bed I still saw the picture that showed Jesus in red clothes and with naked feet. Cripples with crutches under their arms held out deformed hands to the Saviour. The paralyzed man still lay there on his bier; his hands were emaciated and shriveled, and he could not raise them to Jesus; not so much as a finger could he lift. But the Saviour was still turned toward the helpless sufferers; he was stretching out his arms under the red

38

mantle and holding them in blessing over their heads:
JESUS HEALS THE SICK

"You shall have the watch in memory of him," said
Father. "Take good care of it!"

And my brother's watch ticked away in my hand
with desperate haste, as if it had to get somewhere at a
certain time and was late.

Beside Sigfrid's bed stood the chest of drawers.
From one of the drawers Father took his razor, and
from the table the devotional book *Arndt's True Christianity*. He used to shave every Sunday morning, and
now began to strop the razor on the worn, shiny binding of *Arndt's True Christianity,* as he always did.

When it was stropped, Father plucked a hair from
his head and tested the blade on it. It cut the hair
through. He then went into the kitchen and fetched a
towel, soap and a coffee cup of hot water. He was pre-
paring his shaving things.

But he had not fetched the shaving mirror. He was
not going to use the razor on himself.

Father took the shaving things to Sigfrid's bed: "I'll
do this job first."

Mother had sunk down on a chair a step or two from
the bed. She was drawing heavy, laborious breaths. She
had been silent since Father had said that it was
twenty minutes past seven, but now at last she spoke:
"Not going to do it yourself, are you?"

"Who else, then?"

"We could send for someone—for the tailor's son.
He shaves *and* cuts hair."

But Father shook his head. He stirred the shaving
brush round in the soapy water in the coffee cup until it
lathered, standing tall and broad of back beside my
brother's bed. He was at the age when he still had all

39

the strength of manhood. On that Sunday morning he was only forty-odd years old.

And Father was to live for nearly another forty. In 1949 when I came home to see him, I myself had grown-up sons. But now I see myself as the child I was then when my father stood hale and strong at his eldest son's bedside, with a razor in his hand.

He said, "Can do it myself all right."

"How you've got the heart to!" said Mother. "That's what I can't make out."

"Just have to force yourself."

Father bent over my brother and started lathering his face. Sigfrid had got thin and hollow-cheeked that summer, but he had a stiff beard; it grew early on him. From the age of sixteen he had shaved twice a week; for three years he had had a man's growth. I had last seen him shave the day before yesterday, Friday morning. Sigfrid often grumbled about his tough beard, and said that his razor hurt him. But today he was shaved with Father's own sharp, well-stropped blade, and I saw how smoothly it cut. It didn't hurt.

I squeezed Sigfrid's watch hard in my hand. Father had given it to him the year he studied with the pastor: it was a confirmation present. My brother was fifteen then; he had had it for four years. The watch had ticked every second of the time since then, from May, 1908, when he was confirmed, until this July morning, 1912, when summer was at its height. The watch in my hand had measured out four years of a young man's life—until this morning, at twenty minutes past seven.

Sigfrid was carefully shaved today; Father went over his face twice. With the towel he wiped away the lather from cheeks and lips, meticulously. Afterward he stropped the razor once more on the leather-bound

40

devotional book, took out his shaving mirror and began to lather his own face. This was Sunday, and shaving day for him too.

There was a lot to see to now, Father said: "We must think about the urgent things."

He spoke to Mother: "Don't suppose you've got the heart for it?"

"For what?" said Mother.

"Getting him ready."

"No. No. I haven't."

"No. That's what I thought." Father pondered a little before adding, "So we must send for somebody— somebody to wash and shroud the corpse."

Mother looked up with a start: "The *corpse?*" she repeated.

She pushed the word out, hoarsely and violently. It sounded like a fierce rebuke.

"Yes," he said.

"Why d'you say *corpse?*" demanded Mother sharply. "Why not *Sigfrid?*" Mother clutched at her breast as if she had been stabbed.

Father stretched the skin of his neck as he shaved it, and drew the razor over his Adam's apple, which moved up and down under the blade's edge. He cleared his throat and was ashamed. "Of course I . . . only meant . . . well, *you* know."

He was unable to explain what he had meant or hadn't meant. But like Mother, I wanted to ask why he hadn't called Sigfrid by name. Why had he said . . . ? I too had been stabbed by his word. My throat tightened.

Mother went on, "You sound heartless."

"I'm not heartless. Just because I . . ."

Father gaped to get at the stubble at the corners of

41

his mouth, and finished shaving. And while he dried his cheeks and put away his shaving things, he turned again to Mother: He just wanted to talk about what had to be done at once—the most urgent things. Whatever happened to anybody, certain things had to be seen to at once—you couldn't get away from it, nobody could get away from it. There was always something people were forced to do, and somebody had to do it. It was Sunday, and he was going to hurry to church and tell the pastor before service started. It was still early, only half past seven, so he ought to make it. But he must hurry; there was never time enough.

I had heard Father say this often: "There's never enough time!" He always moved hurriedly, and half ran when he walked. Seldom did I see him move in a leisurely fashion, like other people.

In my hand my brother's watch was ticking—hurriedly. In desperate haste it measured out our time in seconds and minutes. Father hurried, the watch hurried, but time itself was never enough. No hour or moment was long enough.

And now Sigfrid was to be got ready.

I struggled to keep up with what was going on. I had never known such a moment as this, or such happenings. Ten minutes might have elapsed since I had got out of bed, but it was still some time before I realized what it was all about. My parents talked of what had to be done now, and who was to do it; and all of it seemed to concern my brother, who was to be got ready.

"Where shall we put him?" Father wondered.

Mother did not answer the question. Instead she said, "We can see ourselves in Sigfrid. See ourselves— like in a looking glass."

42

Father answered, "Got to put it out of your head. Got to try."

I was to put it out of my head too, Father told me. But Sigfrid's watch was now suddenly mine. How had this come about? How? Why was the watch mine?

Because—and it dawned on me what had happened just now, when Father said, "Exactly twenty past seven." I understood, I grasped it with a child's capacity. I had been given Sigfrid's watch and I knew what had happened to him.

I was shaken to the heart. And then at last it came; one couldn't call it crying—the word is inadequate. Water poured from my eyes in fast-falling drops, and that was to be expected, but out of my mouth came sounds that drowned my parents' conversation. It was howling, bawling, an ear-splitting noise. I bellowed so loudly that my sisters stirred in their beds.

"Save us!" exclaimed Mother. "He'll wake the others."

"Better get him out," said Father.

"Yes," said Mother. "That'll be best." Her voice was strangely hoarse.

"He shouldn't have been here for it."

"No, no," said Mother. "But there it was—he woke up."

Then Father spoke to me, and his voice was as severe as it always was when he gave me orders: "Now, lad! Take the cows to pasture!"

Father had told me what to do, and I had to obey.

I rushed out and ran to the cow shed. I let out our cows, drove them along the track, put up the hurdle after them and shut them into the paddock. For this morning job was among the "urgent things"—the things that always had to be done.

I stayed out in the meadow for half the day, just wandering about. I was alone, without other company than our cows. But I didn't want to go back.

While I was down in the meadow my brother was got ready, and when I went home later in the day he was no longer in his bed. He was up in the loft. He and I were no longer to sleep in the same room.

I was barely fourteen when this Sunday morning came; I had never seen anybody stop living. I didn't know what happened when our life here on earth came to an end, and I witnessed it all unprepared.

That was how we parted. My sisters had slept through it. But I had been there when my parents lost their elder son. I had watched my only brother die.

❀❀❀❀

THAT WAS SUNDAY, July 28, 1912. Today is July 24, 1962. Half a century, all but four days, has passed since then.

My brother's watch ticked on in my keeping. It continued for another seven years. After that the movement was worn out and couldn't be repaired. Other watches have reckoned hours, days and years for me; their hands have moved round the dial and measured drops of time from the inexhaustible fountain; they have amassed them all into half a century. But I still have Sigfrid's watch among my private possessions. I have obeyed my father and taken good care of it.

Where the dead are there is no time. Sigfrid remains in the place that he entered fifty years ago. Inaccessible. Nothing has happened to my brother since a certain Sunday morning in July, 1912, when the time was twenty minutes past seven.

Yet I still follow the course of time on my wristwatch and on the wall calendar in my hotel room. I have known fifty annual cycles since then, and much has happened to me. For the ghost in the legend, who attended the wedding of his dead friend, a hundred years went by with each dance, and when he returned he had been away only a short time. I feel the same when I go back: How can fifty years have gone by?

But a moment ago, Sigfrid and I were resting by the brook; I have been away only a little while.

Drops have fallen from the fountain of time, the second hand has ticked, hours have struck and accomplished the cycles of day and night. And my life has gone by.

In Pine Beach we are approaching the hottest time of the year. August and September are the holiday months. The sun scorches; the treeless slopes of the hills turn more russet from the burned grass. But the heat beyond those hills is of quite a different kind. In the inland deserts at this time of year the temperature rises to between 104° and 122°. In Death Valley an air temperature of 134° has been officially recorded. How long can a man live in the Valley of Death in that heat?

But here on the coast the sea winds cool our brows, and even during the hottest months the heat is bearable.

Our West Coast, the land of oranges, belongs to a seismic area of the earth. My home between town and sea stands on volcanic foundations. On occasion the inmates of the Pacific Hotel are given a reminder of the uneasy ground beneath the houses of Pine Beach. But of late years only slight, weak tremors have occurred in these coastal areas, and evoked only fleeting fears among the inhabitants. The last great disaster, in San Francisco in 1906, has been transmuted into a historical event which no one imagines will be repeated.

Yet I am aware of the possibility of waking up some night and finding myself buried under the ruins of the hotel. And I have studied the instructions to be followed in the event of earthquakes: I know what to do when the earth starts to release its seismic energy.

My last occupation was fruit farming, and my days are now spent in winding up the affairs of the orange grove in San Fernando which I sold in the spring. I don't intend to embark on anything else. My business career is at an end. Only a few trifles remain to be settled: I sit here with stacks of papers in front of me. The writing table in my hotel room is so small that there is not nearly enough room for them all; there are always some on the floor.

The Pacific Hotel is designed for people who don't expect luxury, but it does offer reasonable convenience and comfort. The hotel staff have no tinge of the servant about them: they do a job which is regarded as being like any other job, and feel on an equal footing with the guests. In this there is a great difference between America and Sweden. In my own country last summer I found that a sense of shame still clings to such service, so that the employee feels bound to assert himself by being grumpy and disobliging.

My room is small and simple, but holds all I need: a soft, wide bed, an armchair, three other chairs, bookcase and writing table. I have quite a spacious closet for my clothes, but the bathroom is small. In my hotel home I rent my furniture; it doesn't belong to me. I just use it. But it serves me as well as if it were mine. What does it matter who owns the material things I have about me? For a long time I dragged far too much baggage with me on my life's journey, and little by little I have rid myself of it all, except for a few indispensable possessions.

My breakfast is included in the price of my room at the Pacific; lunch and dinner I eat elsewhere. Pine Beach has many little restaurants that serve edible—if not always good—food at a reasonable price. And now

47

I frequent the cheapest places, being obliged to watch my expenditures.

But my body must have its daily nourishment. Today I lunched at Cabrillo's MEXICAN FOOD; there are some cheap dishes on his menu. I ordered tortillas, since the proprietor assured me that they were not too highly spiced. And it was true. Those corn pancakes didn't burn my tongue; in fact they were somewhat too bland for my taste.

The proprietor of MEXICAN FOOD likes to speak of his lineage. Yet it appears to me to be somewhat hazy. Like the rest of us, he is an immigrant to Pine Beach, and has just applied for American citizenship. During the nearly twenty years that I have lived here in the Golden State I have read everything I could find about its history; and now I wanted to test my knowledge of the subject by conversing with the latest-born kinsman of California's Columbus.

Juan Rodríguez Cabrillo, the first white man to set foot on this coast, died three months and five days after his arrival in the new country. He landed here on September 28, 1542, but died of an injury on January 3, 1543, in the Santa Barbara Islands. So I asked Cabrillo how his ancestor could have begotten any heir. Not by any white woman, as there were none here at the time. Had he got some Indian woman with child during his three months' sojourn on this coast? For it was hardly likely that he would have brought any children he might have had in Mexico on this voyage of discovery.

Cabrillo gave only evasive answers to my questions, but violently rejected my hint that there might be some Indian blood in his family: Indian women were quite out of the question. The proprietor of MEXICAN FOOD is

48

a short, dumpy man with a globular head and pitch-black hair, shiny with oil. His teeth are long and sharp, his complexion is very dark and his eyes are deep-set under the arch of his forehead. A man of mixed race who is therefore intensely race-conscious.

He at once abandoned the question of his progenitor and burst into bitter complaint about the municipal authorities. They obstruct him in his activities; they dislike Mexicans and look down on them. There are of course Americans who regard Cabrillo's compatriots as lazy, inefficient and unclean, but the proprietor of MEXICAN FOOD is an exceptionally suspicious man, and I can hardly believe that in this town he can be the victim of discrimination on account of his origins.

As descendant of the first white man ever to set foot in California, he considers he has prior rights over other inhabitants of the town; yet he is obstructed and frustrated at every turn in gaining his legal and lawful livelihood.

And Juan Rodríguez Cabrillo raises his voice: "But madmen and rowdies can do what they like in Pine Beach! Look at that crazy guy who stands out on the street here and bawls out the motorists! They leave *him* alone, all right!"

"You mean Jesus Jensen?"

"That's the one!"

The Mexican shows his powerful teeth in a broad, contemptuous smile: "The Christ fellow! Standing there yelling and holding up the traffic! They put up with *him* all right. But what do they do to Juan Rodríguez Cabrillo? Well, I'll tell you—he gets warnings from the Board of Health!"

I remembered now. A cockroach was said to have appeared on one of Cabrillo's tables in the restaurant, and the customer sitting there had reported the proprietor to the public health authorities.

On my way back to the hotel I met Mrs. Jeffers. She wanted my advice on a complicated housing affair which her firm had just been negotiating. The seller had lied to her about a mortgage—the amount of it—and in all good faith she had passed the lie on to the buyer. The buyer had not checked the sum in question before buying, and now held her responsible, claiming the five thousand dollars that he had been overcharged. But the seller had moved away; she didn't know where he was, and therefore could not claim the money from him. What should she do: pay up, or let the thing come to court? She surely couldn't be made responsible for the five thousand, yet a lawsuit would damage the reputation of her firm.

Mrs. Jeffers was here reviving a phase of my past. It had been full of such problems as she now laid before me: of people's business squabbles, their attempts to pull the wool over each other's eyes, their efforts to cheat legally, to exploit each other's ignorance and trustfulness for gain, and to come by money which they were unwilling to work for. My life as a real-estate man was filled with other people's problems. I fussed with futilities, worried and brooded over them. I dare not now reckon the years of the brief human span that I wasted in that way.

My reply to Mrs. Jeffers is: "I'm sorry, but I can't give you any advice in this business, or in any business. I'm just winding up my own affairs—and I ought never to have been a businessman. I can't imagine now how I could have spent so many years in real estate; I was quite unsuited to it."

I thought my reply would have jolted Mrs. Jeffers,

chief of the biggest real-estate office in Pine Beach. But she just laughed.

"Oh, Mr. Carlson! You *are* cheerful today!"

She thinks I'm joking. She hasn't found out that in her business she lives behind bars. She likes it there. For Mrs. Jeffers the real-estate business is a vocation. She told me so: "To arrange sales and leases for people—to find homes for them—is a fine life's work." And she does all she can to fulfill it.

If I let Mrs. Jeffers believe I am fooling, I can go on being serious. And I am perfectly sincere in saying, "I took the wrong turn in my life—I suppose by a combination of circumstance and my own weakness. I aimed at the nearest targets—easiest to hit. In the very beginning I had a goal that was far more distant; now I see that I should have stuck to that and not tried for anything else. The dream of my youth was to be a man of learning, a historian."

"Oh, a teacher, Mr. Carlson? A professor?"

"No, I didn't want that. I wanted to devote myself to learning for one reason only: I wanted to *know*."

Again Mrs. Jeffers laughs. "Well, who doesn't?" What *she* wants to know is how to cope with this frightful mortgage affair. She is just on her way to her lawyer to get some advice.

We part in the street, in a state of mutual understanding: "To know how to act—that's what we all need most."

As for me, I have arrived at this conclusion: Throughout my life I have been quite incapable of foreseeing the consequences of my actions; they have always turned out quite differently from what I expected.

My emigration, my many years as a prisoner of busi-

51

ness, both my unfortunate marriages—these have been the decisive events of my life.

They all came about through my own decisions, my own actions. Where did they all lead to? To the lonely man in the hotel room, who at the end of his life asks himself whether he regrets them.

But of all forms of self-torment, regret is the most futile. During the time that yet remains to me, I will devote myself to something else.

❦

I go back to my hotel to write a letter to my son Albert, whose birthday is on the last day of July. He moves around a good deal and I have heard nothing from him for a year. I've been waiting for a letter. I don't know where he is at the moment, but I write to the last address I had from him. The letter will probably have to be forwarded, and so I am writing it in good time before his birthday.

This morning I heard from Annie, my second divorced wife, who lives in San Francisco, where she married again. She was a schoolteacher in Carmel when we married. She wonders how I'm getting along and how my attempts at fruit farming turned out. I shall answer: "I began to cultivate the good, wholesome fruits of the earth, thinking that this enterprise would suit me better than any other in this orange-tree state. But I failed partly because of slumps in the fruit market, partly because of bad luck." Bad luck indeed! My last orange harvest was ruined by falls of snow and wintry cold in February, a misfortune that hits the fruit growers of California once in twenty years. My golden fruit ended up on the ground, covered with snow.

52

It was then that I made up my mind to get out. I shall not try anything else. I shall tell my ex-wife that my business career has ended in failure, and she will reply, "I thought it would. I've told you before, you ought never to have become a businessman."

My marriage to Annie lasted only three years. I was her second husband. We had no children, and this has helped us to remain good friends after our divorce. Eight years have passed since we parted, but we write to each other regularly and sign our letters "your friend as always."

But with my first wife, who lives in Gladstone, Michigan, I have no communication. After three unanswered letters to Esther I stopped writing, and I know nothing of her life beyond what I hear from our two sons.

Esther has borne two children, and now she hates their father. It is more than twenty years since our marriage was dissolved and we left each other, but she still hates me. She never sends me a word, not even a greeting through our children. Anyone who can hate with such force and endurance must be an unhappy person. But my sympathy with Esther is mingled with the pangs of conscience: she hurt me, but I hurt her even more.

If I wrote to tell Esther about my failure as a fruit farmer, she would be gleeful: "What did I tell you?" When I left her she predicted that I should do badly— just because I was leaving her. Yes, if I wanted to please my ex-wife I would tell her of my final failure as businessman and boss.

Esther's and my marriage ended in tragedy because we had different ideas as to how people should use their lives here on earth: surely the most valid reason for divorce that can arise in any marriage.

And we shall never meet again.

✤

In my separation from another person who was very close to me the circumstances are entirely different.

I have lived on to this day, but my brother Sigfrid had no more than begun his life when it was taken from him. For fifty years he has been outside time. But he has come back to me. Now he remains with me and I with him.

Here between town and ocean is where I dwell in the physical sense, but I live in the place where I was born. I cannot return to my origins like a ghost. I cannot go back as an old man. But I can do it as child and youth.

And that return shall be my refuge from my awareness, my insight.

WITH SIGFRID'S DEATH my childhood came to an end. When death came to my brother it came close to me too; it forced its way into the room where I slept. It woke me one day without warning; it took me by surprise mercilessly and with a hard hand.

What had happened to my brother might happen to me.

My life in the safe world of childhood was over. Until then I had enjoyed the child's privilege of innocence, which gives him the power of living in the present. I had nothing in the past to regret, for the future I felt only expectation, and I was content with my present. This is what I call happiness. I could not imagine that life would continue to be anything but what it was—I thought it would always be like this.

As a child I knew that death existed, but it didn't concern me. It might concern others, but not me. It lay outside the world in which I moved.

Only once had it come within it, but that had been long before—five years— and I had had time to forget it. A child mourns desperately but not for long, and in childhood five years is an endless expanse of time. Yet Death had once broken in like a robber and taken living creatures from Sigfrid and me—creatures that were our own and to which we were deeply attached.

On our farm we had cows, calves, sheep, pigs, and

poultry, which gave us milk, butter, beef, mutton, pork, wool and eggs. But these were animals found on every farm. For us children they were tiresome creatures, and we took no pleasure in tending them. We also had an old dog, Jäger, a mongrel hunting dog. Jäger was slow at the hunt now, and mostly lay idling the hours away. He was not a playful animal, and we children could well have done without him, but Father hadn't the heart to kill him.

Sigfrid and I wanted animals that were fun, and during the spring when I was in my second year at school and Sigfrid in his last our wish was fulfilled. A boy in the neighboring village raffled his rabbits. Between us we bought a ticket for twenty-five öre—what today would be about a dime—and had marvelous luck. We won a doe of the Blue Beaver strain: the breed that was reputed to be the largest of any. And our prize proved as big as a full-grown hare. But we were the more delighted in that the prize was to increase: the Blue Beaver doe was with young! And rabbits might have as many as fifteen at a birth.

We knocked a rabbit hutch together out of old bits of board, and made it large enough to accommodate the expected increase. From the glass panes of a broken stable lantern we made windows which we set in along the sides of the hutch. In short, we prepared a well-lit and comfortable home for our Blue Beaver, which had cost us only twenty-five öre.

For the first time we had a live creature of our own; and there was joy in tending living things.

We helped each other to feed our rabbit, gathering for her the first spring grass and green leaves, and mixing oatmeal gruel. Twice a day we changed the water in her drinking trough—an old anchovy can—so that it might always be fresh. And our Blue Beaver was content and easily fed. She seemed to like her home. Gently we lifted her by the ears, scratched the back of her neck and stroked her fine blue fur that felt so soft and smooth. She liked being lifted by the ears.

The last thing we did before leaving for school and the first thing on our return in the evenings was to look into the hutch.

As the great event that was to take place in that hutch approached, our excitement and expectancy intensified. We prepared a bed for the new babies with straw and chaff; later the mother herself would line it with fur torn from her own coat.

When the young ones grew up they were to be let out into a playground. We made a hole and a shutter at one end of the hutch, and fitted it with latch and hinges; the hinges were of leather from worn-out shoes. The shutter could be opened like a door when the rabbits went in and out. The run was to be fenced in with wire.

We were to share the young between us, Sigfrid and I, and each take half the litter. Soon I should have my very own rabbits. I studied rabbit breeding in the newspaper, and made great plans for the future.

And one morning when we came out to the hutch the miracle had happened. There was movement among the chaff and straw in one corner, and there lay tiny, pink, hairless bodies that looked as if they had been peeled. A clump of thin-skinned creatures crawled among tufts of fur from their mother's coat; they lay embedded in a soft blue cloud of wool. We saw no eyes; the babies were blind. We picked them up and held them in our hands; how warm they felt, our newborn babies! We counted them: there were eight! To make quite sure we counted them a second and third time, and there were still eight!

That was a big litter, and of a number that could be divided evenly between two. We each counted our baby rabbits and laughed, wild with joy.

That morning we were late for school. Our explanation that our rabbit had had eight babies was not accepted by the schoolmistress; if our rabbit had had a thousand babies it would not have excused us from school. Our punishment was being kept in for half an hour after school that evening.

Of all my six years at the village school that was the slowest school day I remember, and the last half hour the longest. I studied the catechism and Bible history; but what were Moses and Paul, who died long ago, compared with my four live baby rabbits in the hutch? And today—just this very day, when I yearned so desperately to get back to them—I was kept in.

They became even dearer to me because I had suffered on their account.

We counted them again when we got home; there were still eight. Sigfrid worked out how long they would take to grow. Of the eight we each had two pairs, for there were four bucks and four does, and if every doe had eight young, then this very summer we should have thirty-two between us! In the autumn they would increase to sixty-four, and after that to a hundred and twenty-eight, two hundred and fifty-six, five hundred and twelve, and so on. However Sigfrid worked it out, by next spring we should have over a thousand rabbits! I could already see our farm swarming with them, a horde of Blue Beavers scampering over the ground. I saw our fields and paddocks covered with a blue sea of rabbits.

Newborn rabbits are as blind and naked and ugly as kittens, but they soon grow pretty. The eyes of our little Beavers opened, their ears lengthened and thick fur covered their bodies. In a few weeks they were hopping about in the hutch. Sigfrid and I stood for hours on end watching them, and we could see how they grew daily. Soon we had to make their playground and let them out into the fenced run.

One day on our way home from school we decided it was time to divide up our property and make a second hutch.

But when we got home it had happened. How it happened we could never quite make out, but somehow the shutter with the leather hinges had come open. It was open when we got there; the babies had come out, and in the hutch sat the mother, alone.

Four of the little Beavers we found at once. Their bodies lay on the ground near the hutch, bloody, torn, crushed, lifeless. We beheld the work of a wild beast's fangs. The babies had been bitten to death. The mother was still in the hutch, munching away at her dandelion leaves, quite unmoved by the murder of her young ones.

Four were missing, and we started to search for them, hoping they had escaped the Murderer. We looked under every gooseberry bush, in every heap of stones, in every imaginable hole and hiding place. We crawled under the floors of cow shed and barn; we searched in the cellar and in sheds and outhouses. We found nothing, dead or alive.

But we came upon Jäger, our old hunting dog, dozing in the sun at the doorstep. We noticed that he seemed unusually content. His head rested on his outstretched forelegs; his back legs were extended the other way, and his eyes were closed. He lay there comfortably at the top of the steps, replete, satisfied and at ease. Now and again he opened his jaws and sighed with contentment and repletion.

We looked no further for our four missing baby rabbits.

That day, I believe, I cried more passionately than at any other time in my childhood. Something had happened which I had never dreamed could happen—which simply ought not to happen—something that simply should not be allowed to happen. The nine-year-old was cut and outraged to the heart. What I took care of was mine and only mine—my own and nobody else's—and no one should take it from me. What I owned I ought to be allowed to keep. And yet creatures that I had become fond of had suddenly been taken away from me—and I would never get them back, for they were gone forever.

The child had come up against the irrevocable, which he could not grasp, did not want to grasp, and with which he neither could nor would be reconciled. How should a nine-year-old resign himself to so great an injustice?

Sigfrid said, "I'll thrash that cur to death!"

And he went off and cut a thick birch rod. But before he could use it, Father intervened: What was the good of beating the dog? He had done no more than any other dog would do to tender young rabbit flesh moving under its nose: got his teeth into it. And Father didn't think that Jäger had eaten the missing rabbits, merely hidden them after the kill. To us it was all the same. And then Father added that we had only ourselves to blame: We should have fixed a stronger latch to the hutch door.

To whip the Murderer would be useless; no one could restore stolen life.

Beneath a big elm down in the paddock we dug a grave for the dead babies and replaced the turf tidily above them.

And in those days I thought a great deal about death.

Men have tried to picture the appearance of the power that is to take life away from them. They have portrayed that power. They have seen it in various forms. The adversary whom no one can overcome has revealed itself to them. They have seen Death embodied as a man, as a living creature. He has appeared as the harvester with the scythe; as the skeleton with the hourglass; as the rider of the skeleton horse; as the youth with the wings of a bird and the torch; and as the Devil in the shape of a lion. In their imagery Death has assumed the figure of the hunter, the fisherman, the ferryman, and the monster with black bat wings: man and beast in one.

At the age of nine I did not know how others thought of Death. But I now had my own conception: For me Death had become the head of a dog, with gaping jaws.

I had read a story called "The Jaws of Death." It had sprung to my mind when I saw our hound lying at the top of the steps, yawning, dozing, satiated. For me Death became gaping jaws lined with ferocious fangs that tore living creatures to pieces. It became The Jaws of Dog.

Those jaws had all live things in their power: myself, my brother, my parents, all mankind and all the animals. They lay in wait for us all. In those insatiate jaws we should be crushed.

I bared my heart to Sigfrid, and asked him to explain about our dog. We had had him as long as I could remember. He was very old—it seemed he would never die—and no one was willing to put an end to him, not even Father. How could this be? Was Jäger a dog under no one's authority? An everlasting dog? A dog that couldn't die? Couldn't die *because he was Death itself?*

Sigfrid laughed at my contemplative fantasies about The Jaws of Dog. No! No mongrel ruled men. Men ruled dogs.

"I'll show you," he said. "You just wait!"

He sounded mysterious; he was working something out. He was afraid of Father, and therefore cautious. But he promised to show me.

And he did.

It was a Sunday morning. Father and Mother and our sisters had driven to church, and Sigfrid and I were alone at home. He came and took me by the arm, and told me in a low, tense voice that everything was ready; if I would come with him, he would show me something at the top of the steps.

And there lay an empty sack—a big potato sack—that he had hunted out. In his hand Sigfrid held a meaty bone.

I didn't know what was to happen: "What are you going to do?"

"I'll show you!"

Jäger was lying in his kennel. Sigfrid went and lured the dog out with the bone.

"Come on! Let's go down to the stream—to Big Pool!"

He took the empty sack over his arm, while Jäger jumped all around him, trying to get at the bone. Down we went to the stream with the dog at our heels. I said not a word. I dared not ask my brother what he was going to do, yet I guessed at things which both fascinated and scared me: What should we be going to Big Pool for, if not to—?

We crossed the water meadow where there was a bend in the river, and stopped at a grove of willows just beside the pool. On Sundays this place was quiet and private. The water lay shiny, glittering in the sun. In the middle of the pool there was said to be a depth of twelve feet.

Sigfrid said, "Now you must help me."

I had guessed right. In Big Pool Father often drowned kittens in a knotted sack in which he had put stones. The water here was quite deep enough.

Sigfrid was now going to show me that Jäger's jaws could do no harm to us people; but we ourselves could destroy the jaws of Death. *We ruled over Death*. People in fairy tales always did this—in the end.

The Jaws of Dog should take no more lives from us.

Yet I was afraid. All at once my throat felt so constricted and my tongue so thick that I couldn't utter a word. I was about to help with something that I had never done before. I had watched animals die, I had seen them slaughtered, but I had merely looked on; I had taken no part in the killing. Now I was to help, and that was something very different. I was ashamed to show my brother that I was terrified.

Sigfrid called Jäger, and then we each took hold of the mouth of the sack. My hands were trembling. Sigfrid let Jäger sniff at the bone, and then tossed it into the sack.

But the dog would not go in. He looked at us as if in suspicion—as if he guessed that we meant him no good. Why should he get into the sack? Jäger was an intelligent animal, and not one to walk voluntarily into a trap.

We tried to drag him into the sack, but he kept resisting. Not until our third attempt did we succeed. Sigfrid caught hold of the dog's collar and hauled. I felt weak all over. Our old dog had fought against this so desperately.

Sigfrid tied up the mouth of the sack with a long, strong cord. And all of a sudden I was inside the fairy tale: we had imprisoned Death!

But how stupidly we had gone about it! Too hastily, I knew—we had forgotten something.

"Oh, hell!" Sigfrid exclaimed. "We must have stones in there or it won't sink!"

He told me to hold on to the sack while he went down to the shore for stones, not noticing how terrified I was or how my hands were shaking.

I nearly cried out to him, "No—I can't hold on—I can't!" For the sack had suddenly come to life. It was a living bundle that I held in my unsteady hands—a bundle in violent motion, jerking, tossing itself about, rolling back and forth. The sack began moving over the ground; I had to let go. It was snatched from my grasp, it dragged itself along, stumbled on kicking feet, jumped up and down, somersaulted and rolled away over the grass.

From inside the bundle came piercing yelps.

All round me on the ground crawled a living thing of the color of sackcloth—a grayish-brown, hairy animal. Now it rolled, now it moved in jumps and jerks. Its head was the ruffled end of a tied-up sack on a thin, corded neck. From the neck hung long ends of cord that whipped to and fro, as from the throat of a strangled person, a man hanged.

The sack-beast crawled about and tumbled and uttered pitiful howls and screams. And now the screams were coming from my own mouth too—the cry of a frightened child.

Sigfrid came running back from the stream. "What's the matter? What are you yelling for?"

I couldn't answer. And there was no need to say anything, or explain. Sigfrid himself now saw the sack that had come alive and was rolling about. Inside it was a life that kicked out wildly, threw itself here and there and rolled and went head over heels—a prisoner in bonds, trying frantically to free himself.

And didn't he see also that a miracle had suddenly come about? This grayish-brown sack-beast! It moved, it crawled among the bushes, creeping at random, for it was blind—a creature without eyes.

Sigfrid asked no more questions: he just stood and watched.

It had seemed to me that we had trapped The Jaws of Death in our potato sack. Instead we had shut in a living being which itself was fighting against Death. And the noise from inside the sack was like a human cry.

Sigfrid heard it too; he both saw and heard.

The crawling, squealing sack-animal was blind, and saw no obstacles in its path over the ground. It never saw the big osier bush that spread out its branches ahead. One of these branches grabbed the long, dangling cords of the neck, and the animal entangled itself and stuck fast in the osier. The more it struggled and rolled, the more entangled it became and the more firmly it stuck.

The monster was caught by the osier. There it lay helpless, unable to get free of it. Yet it went on struggling as violently as before. Four legs went on kicking, and the pitiful noise inside the sacking never stopped.

Sigfrid's face had paled. He may have been as frightened as I was. "Oh, God, I can't do it—I can't—no!"

These were the words that I too wanted to cry out.

I dared not touch that kicking, screaming bundle over there; nothing could have induced me. But Sigfrid went over to the osier and released the sack-beast. He freed it from the branches and undid the cord round the neck; he undid all the knots and opened the sack.

Out shot the dog as if he had been hurled. Our old hunting dog set off for home as swiftly as a yearling, and in a few moments was out of sight. Never had I seen him run like that.

The monstrous sack-beast that had come alive at my feet was gone. My terror loosened its hold.

Picking up the potato sack, Sigfrid folded it slowly and carefully and put it under his arm.

"No!" he said. "No—I'll have nothing to do with death. Never."

I had thought we had tied Death up in the sack. Now Sigfrid had undone the sack again and opened it. But it was not Death that he had set free: *it was a life*.

When we left Big Pool we agreed that nobody should ever know what we had tried to do that Sunday. And we never talked about it to each other afterward.

What we had done we would never do again. And

Sigfrid had said that he would have nothing to do with death.

In the autumn of that year Jäger ate some poisoned meat that had been put out for the fox, and he died of it. Our harrier was suddenly absent. The Jaws of Dog had taken their own life by greedily swallowing the piece of meat they found in the woods. After that it became easier for me to forget the gaping maw into which living creatures disappeared: the horror of death released its hold on me.

Five years passed before that Sunday morning when it returned.

Under the big chestnut at the end wall of the cottage stood a bench where Sigfrid and I used to sit on warm summer evenings. The last time we sat there together was one Friday evening during the haymaking season. Suddenly he said that he felt tired, and would go to bed. He got up and went, but had taken only a few steps when he turned and asked whether we should go to the stream next Sunday. "Yes," I said, "if you feel up to it." Then he left me. It was still early in the evening and I didn't want to go to bed yet, so I took a walk down by the ploughland.

Sigfrid never said anything more to me. And I sat no more on the bench under the chestnut that summer.

My brother had gone from me without saying good-bye. The one to whom I was most closely bound had left me and would never come back.

Sigfrid was carried up to the loft where we stored the grain, where he lay on a plank supported by two chairs, which had been placed on the newly swept floor. Father had called him the corpse; but so long as he remained in the house I couldn't really believe that he was dead.

It had been difficult to get him up the narrow, crooked stairway to the loft, but he still belonged to our house; he still lay under the same roof with me. The difference between us was that he was no longer breathing. But I had read about suspended animation. Perhaps he only seemed to be dead. Might he wake up and start breathing again? Might he even come back? He couldn't go away from me so suddenly, and stay away.

On the morning of the funeral I saw him for the last time. There he lay in the coffin, which was set on trestles in the yard. There was no lid to it; the funeral party was to look at him. His face had altered; it was sunken, smaller, and the closed eyes lay deeper under his forehead. But he lay as still as before. There was no movement in his chin, no breath in his body. He did not awaken and sit up.

Yet I would not relinquish my hope that he might be in a trance. When they came to put the lid on the coffin, I was on the point of shouting, "No! Don't do it! He'll be smothered! He'll be smothered! Don't!"

But I looked on silently; quietly I watched what was going on. And my throat tightened as if I myself were being cut from air and light by a black lid.

There was sunshine; it was a bright, clear morning brilliant with summer. Greenery and the scent of grass surrounded us in the farmyard as we stood there in a group about the black coffin. People were saying what fine weather it was for getting in the hay.

But I breathed the light air of the morning heavily. And when they had screwed down the lid of Sigfrid's coffin, I could only hope that he was not in a trance.

For a long time after the funeral I felt that my brother could not have gone forever. One fine day he would come back to us. I had read in the Bible of dead people being restored to life. At school I had learned how Jesus could raise up the dead; it was done quickly and simply. Why couldn't He give my brother back his life, when it was so easy for Him to do it? And in my evening prayers I asked Jesus to wake Sigfrid back to life as he had done with Lazarus and the widow's son in Nain. As an extra petition in the Lord's Prayer I prayed God to let His Son do one more miracle, just one more.

But Jesus did not give me what I asked for. Wouldn't He or couldn't He? Which? Why should He not hear my prayer? The only reason must be that He couldn't do it. And then I began to think that I had been taught lies at school. He who was called the Son of God had no power over Death. Jesus could not bring Sigfrid back to life, any more than God Himself could.

Under the picture JESUS HEALS THE SICK I had seen my brother draw his last breath. And now neither God nor His Son heard my prayers when I asked that he might be given back his life. There could be but one explanation: Who does not exist can not hear. Our Father was not in heaven, His Son had never been on earth. God could not have a son, because He did not exist, so there was no point in praying to Him for anything. For Sigfrid there was nothing for it but to stay among the dead, while I was left behind among the living.

During the time immediately following my brother's death I lost the childhood faith that had been implanted in me during six years of school. I gave up saying my prayers.

That autumn I spent my last term at the old village school, which lay beside a large bog far in among the wooded grazing lands. On my first day at school Sigfrid had come with me. We were still living in the crofter's cabin then. It was a cold, snowy winter's day. We walked along the narrow, winding woodland track—the

70

lumbermen's road, our road to school. I was seven years old, I was little, I walked beside my big brother and he held my hand. The track was snowed under that morning, and the drifts were so deep that I had to hold on to Sigfrid so as not to tumble into them. I was very frightened. I was to enter a new world where there were many strange children—big, strong boys who always wanted to fight, and always threatened to thrash the smaller boys. When we came near the schoolhouse and I heard the din from the playground, my eyes filled with tears. My nose was running too, but no doubt that was from the cold. Sigfrid said, "Now, don't you start sniveling! And wipe your nose before we go in!"

For two years I went to school with my brother, and during that time I had no need to fear the big boys who liked fighting. But when Sigfrid finished his schooling I had no one to protect me from them. I had to submit to the stronger ones, for fear of a beating.

But during my last school year I was a big, strong fourteen-year-old, and needed to fear no other boy. There was no boy bigger and stronger than myself.

After losing my childhood faith I was not afraid even of God any longer. What could He do to me when He didn't exist? I could do things I had never dared to do before. I did not obey my parents as I used to, and I defied the schoolmistress. Sometimes I argued with her. During a catechism lesson I asked her about original sin: Was it fair that parents should escape punishment for their sins by leaving them for their children to inherit? Was it fair that innocent little children should suffer for what grown-ups had done?

Our schoolteacher was much upset; she took me aside, called me a blasphemer and asked what had come over me. Until now she had felt no anxiety about

71

me, and on the whole I had behaved well. Now in my last term I had grown defiant and impudent. This was the more extraordinary in that I had just suffered a bereavement: my only brother had died young. This should have made me serious and God-fearing. God sent us trials and sorrows for our own good, that we might be made better by them. Yet I had deteriorated, I was hardening. My only brother had been snatched away, but I took no warning from it.

The teacher held up my brother Sigfrid as an example to me. He had never disobeyed her. How happy she would be if all her pupils were like him! Sigfrid— there was a boy for other boys to emulate!

I blurted, "Then why wasn't he allowed to go on living?"

At this insolent question our teacher was appalled. I was kept in for two hours after school.

But Sigfrid had not been the model boy the schoolmistress thought him. He was guilty of many pranks that she would have punished him for if she had known of them. But he was never openly disobedient and committed his misdeeds without being caught. He had the best head of all those forty children; he hardly had to study his lessons at all and seemed to know them already. He could learn long passages from his books by heart in quite a short time, and his head for figures astonished everybody. In our arithmetic book there were some difficult problems that even the schoolteacher was unable to write down and work out, but Sigfrid could.

I was a lazy pupil. Most subjects in the curriculum were a torment to me, and worst of all were the catechism and Bible history. But the history of my own country I loved; of that book I could repeat a great deal by heart, and was the best in the school in the subject. This was natural: I meant to write history books myself when I grew up.

I had been warned and sternly admonished by the schoolmistress, but I continued to defy her. I misbehaved in class, I did forbidden things during recess. I began to use swear words. And I did the thing that was most strictly forbidden of any: I learned to play cards.

A few of us boys used to sneak out during the rest periods into the paddock beyond the playground and play knock, twelves, twenty-one and spoil five. We lay hidden under the bushes. We played with tiny cards— the sort fastened to the chocolate cakes in the local shop. The cards were only an inch long. We never played for money, because we had none. But we were fascinated by the little cards and by the forbidden game, and we spent the whole lunch hour hidden in the paddock.

In the end we were found out. A girl told the schoolmistress, who came and caught us in the act. We defended ourselves by saying that we were only playing with a toy pack. Our cards were so tiny that the sin too must be tiny. Our teacher wept for us, and grieved especially over me because I had set my foot upon the path of sin, although God had warned me by taking my only brother from the world.

Sigfrid and I shared a home where we were brought up in the strict, Old Lutheran faith, in the pure evangelical doctrine. We had to learn to obey God's Ten Commandments, of which the fourth was the foremost: we must honor and venerate our parents and obey their orders. Disobedience to Father and Mother was a great sin and was punished with beating, with the birch rod when we were little and with the cane when we were bigger. And with his large, hard hands Father would cuff me so that my head spun. I would look respectfully at Father's hands at meals, when they held knife and fork: they could hurt.

I understand my parents. They themselves had been brought up in the fear of God; they had obeyed their parents and now we must obey ours. They did what they thought best for their children. They loved us; we were the most precious things they possessed on earth. They mourned their dead children as deeply as any parents can mourn. For them we were a loan from God, and they owed it to Him to take good care of us. They were responsible for both our bodies and our souls; and one day they would have to account to God for the children that He had given them. We were a sacred trust; therefore they must maintain authority over us, and we must obey, honor and venerate them.

It was Mother who watched over us lest we fall into sin. She was the strictest and most serious Christian I've ever met. Like her, Father observed all the Christian customs, attending church every Sunday and taking communion once a month—but, unlike her, he did not carry the teachings and commandments of the Christian faith into the working week; he did not, like her, walk in constant dread of sinning. He was emotional and could be moved to tears by a sermon, but he soon forgot it, and when the working day followed he lived entirely in this life and had no fears about the life to come.

I never let my mother know that I had ceased to believe in God. If I had told her, I would have hurt her very much. I might have explained the whole thing to my father; he would have admonished me, but his consternation at the error of my ways would not have lasted long.

When he was about ten, Sigfrid had once broken both the fourth and the seventh commandments, but Father had been lenient. My brother was in church with Father and Mother; a collection was to be taken for the heathen mission and he had been given a penny to put in the bag. He put his hand into the bag but held on to the coin. On the way home from church he went into Candy-Lisa's store and bought a big paper cornet of sweets with the money. He was careless with it; Mother noticed it and asked where he had got the money to buy sugar sticks with. Sigfrid had to confess that he had bought them with the money that Father and Mother had given to the Christian mission for the spreading of the Gospel. He had stolen, and he had disobeyed his parents. If he had been hungry and had spent this money on bread, they might have overlooked it, said Mother. As it was, she thought he ought to have a switching. But Father pronounced a milder sentence, and let it go with a reprimand and a promise from the boy never to do such a thing again.

Mother had an elder brother, Johannes of Bogesjö, who was a famous village preacher and belonged to a sect known as the Old Readers. One Sunday in summer, when I was about ten, Uncle Johannes was to expound the Bible at our farm. The meeting was to take place in the open, on the level ground in front of the house. We carried out all our chairs and laid planks across them, to provide plenty of seats. Nearly all the villagers came to listen to Johannes, and there were so many of them that some had to sit on the grass. We children of the house were ordered to attend; we were washed and combed and dressed in our best clothes.

That Sunday Sigfrid had found a bird's nest in the old hollow service tree down by the cattle track. The hen bird, which was sitting on her eggs in the hole, had a red back and a long sharp beak. He didn't know what kind it was. She hissed at him like a snake when he peered in. Sigfrid was eager to show me his discovery, and we would gladly have skipped the sermon, but we were compelled to sit and listen to Uncle Johannes.

Sigfrid and I sat somewhat apart from the others, behind the gooseberry bushes. The ground sloped down from the front steps where the preacher took his stand above us. Johannes of Bogesjö was a gigantic, broad-shouldered fellow with thick, brushed-up hair. His powerful voice thundered over the open space and resounded from the house wall behind him; his words echoed from the walls of the farm buildings a couple of hundred yards away. He took as his text Chapter 25, verse 41, of the Gospel according to St. Matthew:

"Then shall he say also unto them on the left hand, Depart from me, ye cursed, into everlasting fire, prepared for the devil and his angels."

Uncle Johannes told us about hell. He described minutely the torments awaiting those who on the last day should be placed on the left hand of Jesus—those whom he would cast out to burn in everlasting fire.

To burn or be burned was the most terrible thing I could imagine. I knew what it felt like, for once a brand had rolled from the fireplace onto my bare foot. I got a smarting burn and tender blisters on that foot. But the pain passed in a few days. Now Uncle Johannes was speaking of fiery pains that had no end: "If we thrust our hands into the flames on the hearth we have had a slight foretaste of what awaits the cursed whom Jesus has driven out. We can withdraw our hand and escape the pain, but the damned cannot. And we should reflect on this: how would it feel to remain in a fire which we cannot escape and which never goes out, and what such endless torment must be like."

The voice of the preacher rolled over the farmyard and echoed among the buildings: "On which side of Jesus will we stand at the Day of Judgment? Those who do not want to stand on the left hand must reform from this hour. Everlasting, everlasting—remember the everlasting torments." The people on the benches, our neighbors and villagers, listened in fear and trembling, with bated breath.

It was a bright June day, and the first summer flowers were in full bloom around us. The lilacs were white, the leaves of the fruit trees gleamed in the sun, bumblebees buzzed in the grass. There was light over the earth. But shudders ran through me where I sat in the midst of this glory, among flowers and grass. An everlasting fire was kindled over it all. I felt again the scorching pain from the firebrand that had fallen on my bare foot. The ground darkened, the green faded, the grass withered away, the flowers vanished and yielded no more scent. Johannes of Bogesjö drove the bright summer day from our farm and invoked hell instead; his voice sounded as if issuing from dark clouds in the sky; he was transforming our bright June day to black doomsday.

The audience was held in mute, submissive devotion. They were silent, scared; they dared not utter a sound. "Without end . . ." The people seemed to have stopped breathing. All eyes were fixed upon the preacher, and from many of them tears were flowing. But the sobs were muffled, stifled—it was a subdued and terrified weeping. Father and Mother wept; Father wiped his tears with the back of his hand, Mother with her apron.

My eyes remained dry, but I wriggled as if something was hurting me. I looked at the preacher's mouth. I knew that Uncle Johannes chewed snuff; chewing was permitted to a Christian, though smoking was a sin. As he spoke, he bared his upper teeth and I could see the black specks of snuff on them. They distracted me from the sermon.

My brother Sigfrid didn't cry either—he made faces instead. He detested Uncle Johannes; he used to make fun of him and mimic his preaching voice.

He whispered, "Come on! Let's get out of here!"

"Dare we?"

"Nobody'll see. Just follow me."

Sigfrid began slowly creeping backward, away from the gooseberry bushes. I went after him. We crawled backward through the long, unmown grass. No one was looking at us; all eyes were on the preacher. When we were hidden behind a big lilac bush, we got up and began running. In no time we were behind the cow shed. No one had seen us sneak away.

It was the red bird in the hollow service tree that enticed us, and we ran down to the cattle track. The nest was high up in the trunk of the tree; we climbed up and tried to peer down into the deep black hole where the bird was sitting. We could see only fiery-red back feathers and a long, black, sharp beak, and hear an angry hissing noise. Like a snake striking, said Sigfrid. What strange bird was this that had nested in the old tree?

We took turns looking into the hole, but couldn't recognize the bird that had laid her eggs there, and soon we left her in peace.

We had run away from doomsday, and the bird's nest had put right out of our minds the Bible talk, the sermon and everlasting torment. A child's happy oblivion. We went down to the paddock and saw that the wild strawberries round the tree stumps were still unripe and would not be red for another week or so. We did not want to go home until the sermon was over.

After a good hour we started back. I wondered whether Uncle Johannes was still there.

Sigfrid said, "There's no such thing as hell. It's just something pastors talk about."

He was fifteen and had read many books; everyone said he had a good brain. I was in the habit of believing all he said.

But I had been rather frightened during the Bible talk that day.

"You mean hell's something they've made up?"

"Of course! Nobody can say where it is."

"It's supposed to be underneath us."

"But where? And if it was, we'd see the smoke from the fire. No. There isn't any hell."

I trusted my elder brother, and his assurance calmed me.

When we got back to our house, the sermon was over and the yard empty. But at the top of the steps stood Father and Mother and Uncle Johannes. My heart sank: they looked as if they were waiting for us.

Johannes of Bogesjö looked at us, his eyebrows drawn sternly together. "Are your boys coming here at *this* hour? Didn't they listen to my sermon?"

"They were ordered to," said Father.

Our uncle turned to Mother, and said in a tone of sadness and grave concern, "You're my dear sister. So I tell you this: On the Last Day you will have to answer for the souls of your young children!"

Mother stood deeply ashamed and conscience-stricken beside her brother, the famous preacher.

"Bear in mind what I say to you, dear sister!"

We had been missed. In our parents' faces we saw what awaited us. We saw what Uncle Johannes demanded of them. And we would have liked above all to run away again.

First Father ordered us to take the chairs back into the house and the planks into the woodshed. Meanwhile Mother prepared food for the preacher, and laid the table for him in the big room where he was to eat alone. When he had gone, Sigfrid and I had to enter in turn and take our punishment for disobeying God's fourth commandment, which said that we should honor our father and mother that it might be well with us and that we might live long on the earth.

Lying face downward at full length on the floor, with my trousers drawn down and a bared bottom, I was given the birch rod. Then my brother in the same position had the cane. I screamed, Sigfrid did not.

Afterward my elder brother had some words of comfort for me: We wouldn't be home sons all our lives!

But I recall only a few occasions when Sigfrid was thrashed for naughtiness. He was his parents' obedient son.

The Bible reading that Uncle Johannes gave at our farm I was to remember well; the memory was revived a couple of years later when my mother fell very ill and Johannes came back to us.

Mother's condition was grave, and sometimes she was delirious. She was believed to have pneumonia. No doctor had even been to our house, and none was sent for now, although there was talk of it. Instead Johannes of Bogesjö came to Mother and sat for long spells with her. He had come in place of the doctor.

Sigfrid and I were out working with Father all day; our sisters looked after Mother.

One evening when I came in I went over to her bed. Her cheeks were red and shiny with fever and sweat, and her hair was sticking to her forehead.

Mother looked at me with bright eyes and said, "Albert, pray to God for me!" There was entreaty in the weak voice. Mother's voice sounded like a child's, and she was speaking to a child, her younger son: "Please, Albert! Pray for your mother like a good boy."

She was very ill; the son that she had brought forth stood by her bed, fit and healthy. Mother was big and grown up and I still little, but she was asking me to help her.

I said I would ask God to make her well again.

"It's not the sickness—that doesn't matter. But my soul. . . . Please, Albert."

Mother had told me the same thing many times before: People shouldn't care what happened to them in this world. And now it was not the disease in her body that frightened her, for that was of this world, and all worldly things passed away. But she was afraid of what might happen to her in another world. Mother wanted me to pray for her soul.

She went to communion every month, she recited the

general confession, she prayed daily that God would forgive her sins; she did everything that was required of a Christian. Yet she did not feel sure of salvation after death; she feared the eternal punishment, the fire that burned and burned but never consumed. I knew that Uncle Johannes had just been with her.

I sensed Mother's fears: I saw them in her eyes, heard them in her voice, felt them in her fever-hot hand when it sought mine.

She took my hand and said that my prayers would help her more than a grown person's, for I was a child. I hadn't had time, surely, to fall into any sin save original sin. A child was more innocent than a grown person, and therefore God opened his ears to prayers from a child's mouth. He listened to such prayers; he would listen to me if I prayed for her.

And I did so that night, after my usual evening prayer. I prayed God that Mother might go to heaven if she died. She had had such a hard life on earth that it was only right that she should have a good time afterward. Three children, my three little brothers, had died and were now with God. And I ended my prayer by saying that Mother ought to be allowed to go to the heaven where her children had gone before her.

But my mother recovered from her illness.

She told me when she left her sickbed that my prayers had been answered, but in a way that God thought best for me. He had thought it happiest for me that I be allowed to keep my mother.

Mother lived for another thirty years, but she never lost her dread of eternal agony. It tormented her for the rest of her life. In a letter to me in America during an illness many years later she repeated in writing to

82

the grown man what she had said to the child: "Please, Albert! Pray to God for me!"

Of hell it may be said that mere belief in it suffices. That belief robbed my mother of the joy of life.

✟✟✟✟

WE ARE WELL into August now. It is the high season and the Pacific Hotel is full up. Vacationers throng Pine Beach, and the shore below my west window is swarming with people who have come to drown their tiredness in the biggest ocean in the world. For most of the year the beach is empty of people, although the water maintains a temperature of about 68°. Americans in general like their sea bathing tepid, but I find it most stimulating when it is under 68°.

Both my windows are open and the sea wind blows coolingly through the room. I am sitting at the writing table, which stands by the east window. The red-scorched hills to the east raise their high shoulders to the blazing sun. I fancy to myself that originally these hills belonged to the ocean; they look like giant waves that have come rolling in from the assembly of waters, to halt and harden on their journey across the earth.

I am dealing with the remainder of my affairs; I make entries and examine accounts relating to the orange grove in San Fernando which is no longer mine. I send in bills and pay debts. I am winding up the last business enterprise of my life. I say goodbye to the blossoming orange trees. My dealings with their fruit are now at an end.

I had bad news in the mail this morning. The export

firm in San Diego, which of recent years has been my biggest customer, has become insolvent owing to the slump in the fruit trade. I shall be forced to accept 30 per cent of my claim in full settlement. This means that my loss on San Fernando will be considerably heavier than I calculated when I sold the business.

I go through the list of consignments to the San Diego firm for the last fiscal year. But my table is not a proper writing table, and there is no room on it for all my papers. Again and again I have to pick up from the floor these papers which have filled my days. A little hotel room without a proper writing table has become my last office: a symbolic end to my commercial career.

Today in the hall of the Pacific I met Mrs. Jeffers. She had been lunching with a customer who through her had bought a house in Long Beach. I saw from her eyes that she had pulled off a successful deal. She told me that she had just had a letter from her husband, who is at present in Montana, where he intends to buy a farm and raise beef cattle. He is sure that this will prove a very profitable undertaking.

I expressed the opinion that land in Montana is better suited to sheep. At any rate there are big sheep farms up there. But Mrs. Jeffers replied that people in this country eat enormous quantities of beef, and that our production so far nowhere near satisfies the demand. We have to eat imported beef. And since the States so badly need meat for its population, a beef cattle farm is bound to be profitable.

Mrs. Jeffers seemed quite exhilarated as she expatiated on the favorable state of the meat market, though she said it was now uncertain whether her husband could come to Pine Beach this autumn as he had planned. This farm project would probably keep him up there in Montana.

But I know that Mr. Jeffers will never come to Pine Beach. I know it through a close friend of Mrs. Jeffers. Husband and wife have been separated for years, without a formal divorce, and have no communication with each other. The wife doesn't even know where her husband is, but for the benefit of her acquaintances in Pine Beach she maintains the fiction "away on business." He will remain away.

I began almost to believe in the husband's Montana farm; Mrs. Jeffers knew so many details about it. She is a successful real-estate lady and might do as well as a fiction writer.

Her real-estate office is a refuge. For Mrs. Jeffers it is the hub of the universe. She is a slave to her business, but cannot do without her shackles. Her affairs help her to live, and I had thought that they sufficed. But now I see that she needs something more— something beyond the office, beyond the buying and selling of houses; something that she herself can create: a husband who starts great new enterprises and founds a farm in Montana for raising beef cattle for meat-eating compatriots.

I too have been the prisoner of the real-estate business. How many times I longed to flee from it, how many times I tried to escape! I had to do violence to my innermost nature to get through my daily work. And now I have begun to wonder how Mrs. Jeffers feels when she opens up her office in the mornings: Would she close it forever if she could? What is there to prevent her? She is alone and free. During my imprisonment in real estate I had to consider my wife, my children, my wife's family, my friends in the town. Today

I find it hard to understand why I did it—why I stayed so long in that business.

Now the day is approaching when I shall be free of all paper work. I sit at my accounts until the room begins to darken. Then I rest for a while; I don't switch on the light, but walk to the east window and look out: my eyes seek a man who should be standing at the intersection, and they find him. Jesus Jensen is at his post.

The Dane is no follower of Jesus; he is not even a Christian. Jesus Jensen is a heathen. The other day I had a conversation with him about religion. I went into a snack bar on Ocean Avenue to eat a hamburger, and on the stool beside me sat the Dane with a glass of orange juice in front of him. The loudspeaker was broadcasting a church service, with sermon and hymn-singing. This irritated Jesus Jensen; he spoke vehemently against all teachings and religions that promise us anything after death. Such treachery toward mankind had always outraged him. Of Christianity he spoke almost blasphemously; indeed he described himself as a blasphemer. But he wanted to protect and preserve human life on earth; through its very transience our existence had infinite greatness, but we had not yet learned to value it and love it as we should. Jesus Jensen wanted to proclaim a new doctrine of love. For the moment he only hinted at it, but said he would develop it in more detail for me another time.

I go out to buy my evening paper at the drugstore. As usual, Mrs. Boles gives me a commentary on the latest news before I have read a word of it. She reads everything that she can find in print about the nuclear tests, and has now discovered that Communist China is to have atomic bombs; this has greatly intensified her fears for mankind. China has the largest population of any country in the world, nearly twice as numerous as America and Russia put together: something like 700,000,000. And if Americans and Russians were to come to their senses in the matter of nuclear weapons, there would still remain the 700,000,000 Chinese.

Mrs. Boles now goes into the matter of the radioactive material that is released when a hydrogen bomb is tested and dropped: strontium 90. It has been scientifically proved, she says, that in human reproduction this material is passed on to the children, causing genetic damage: the most horrible diseases may be inherited through several generations. She cannot find words to express her feelings about this.

I remind her of the words in the Bible about the iniquity of the fathers being visited upon the children unto the third and fourth generation. We were reviving the concept of original sin.

"But this is not a question of everybody's sin," Mrs. Boles objects. "The guilty ones form only a small group. But countless millions of the innocent must suffer."

"The people who bear the heaviest responsibility are the scientists, who have put nuclear weapons into the hands of politicians and soldiers," I remark, handing over my dime for the paper.

She drops the coin into the till, and her face is grim and stern. "If I weren't too old I should study science myself. Learn how to make a hydrogen bomb."

"And what would you do with it, Mrs. Boles?"

"Drop it on the factories that make hydrogen bombs. On those scientists you were talking about."

"Well, it's an idea."

88

"Not many people would have to be wiped out. I should only need a baby bomb."

With that she turns to a new customer at the counter.

❦

I return to the hotel, go up to my room and sit down to my papers again.

I have begun to calculate the losses incurred in the last business enterprise of my life. There follows the question: How long shall I be able to afford to stay here at the Pacific? A few months, perhaps. After that I shall have to find a more modest room, a less comfortable bed, cheaper food. But for the moment I don't want to make plans, and I put aside my worries about the future.

Why should I turn tomorrow into a threat—something to be dreaded? It is not tomorrow that I am living in now, not next week or next month. It's this minute, this hour, this day that I am to get through. The time that is not yet must be accepted when it comes, when I am living in it. That time too will move on, pass from me, and my anxiety about it will pass with it. The morrow that I fear will soon be gone.

So I live on through one day at a time in my hotel room. One day at a time—but it is not enough: here nothing happens to me, I experience nothing. I need to be at one more place on earth. So I find my way to my beginnings, to another region of our earth. There events come to pass in my memory.

Here I am an old man—but in another country I am still a child and a youth.

⚜⚜⚜⚜

SIGFRID AND I WERE PARTED in 1912, but it was the year before, 1911, that my brother's fate was determined. He was to take charge of his own life. That year he was to go out into the world.

There were too many of us at home. Our little holding, a sixteenth of a *mantal*, could not feed all seven of us. And since Sigfrid was the eldest of the brood, he must be the first to diminish it. He was now fully grown; he had overtaken Father in height and was three whole inches taller. He was proud of this and liked us to mention it. My brother was taller than Father, but Father had authority over him so long as he stayed at home. "So long as you eat my bread you'll obey me!" said Father; and none of us dared gainsay him.

Sigfrid himself asked nothing better than to go out into the world. He wanted to get away from home, at whatever cost. He didn't want to be a home son—he hated the very words. "Sounds like one of the livestock," he said to me. He wanted to be independent.

But what was he to do in life? He possessed his healthy body, and that was all. But he could earn his living with it. His strong frame was fit for any hard work.

Yet he was uncertain and hesitant. I was still a child and did not realize then how lost and groping he was. In front of me he pretended to be self-assured; but he had hardly been beyond his home parish and knew nothing of life outside. Since then I have come to understand how Sigfrid felt when he was to go out into the world, an inexperienced, naïve, dreamy young man, alone with his decision: "I can't stay at home any longer! I must get away! But do I know how to use my life?"

In 1911 I was thirteen. Sigfrid had had his eighteenth birthday that spring. His adult life was to begin.

In 1911 we had that dry summer when the wells gave out, the springs failed and fish died in the dried-up hollows of the Bjurbäck.

It was a time of difficulty and hard labor for us on the farm. It was the summer of water carrying. We had far to go for it, and we looked for hidden springs in the outlying pastures. From the pools in the stream we filled casks and drove them back for the stock, and from an old spring far down in the woodland pasture we collected drinking and cooking water for ourselves. Sigfrid and I had the job of fetching it. Water is heavy. We toiled with buckets and pitchers until our backs bent and our arms stretched. And we had to go slowly and cautiously over the stony path through the copse so as not to spill any from the brimming vessels.

Sigfrid could manage three-and-a-half-gallon buckets, one in each hand. For me a one-and-a-half-gallon pitcher in each hand was heavy enough. How we toiled and sweated for water that summer, my brother and I.

Sigfrid was very strong. One evening when we were on our way home from the woodland spring with our water buckets, I tripped over a shiny, slippery fir root, fell and sprained my ankle. I couldn't move a step. But Sigfrid took me on his back and carried me all the long way back to the farm. I clung fast with my arms round his neck, to leave his hands free for his buckets. He carried me on his back and the full pails in his hands, without effort.

I wanted to be as strong as my brother and do all that he could do. I worked at it: I did straight-arm weight lifting, tried to master the holds in wrestling, and practiced target shooting with a crossbow. I learned to "tame steers": My brother and I would tie the ends of the ox reins round our ankles and from a standing position try to pull each other down with our feet. When I managed to get him down I was praised for it, and felt proud.

Sigfrid was my teacher and my model, and the only person in my little world whom I confided in. My sisters played different games from ours and amused themselves alone. To Father and Mother I could talk only of the things that they wanted to talk to me about. Mother might sometimes reveal something of her inner thoughts, but Father was for me a closed, alien person during my growing years. He ruled me, and I was afraid of him. He kept me hard at it. When I came home from school in the afternoons he at once set me to work at some job or other. It was useless for me to plead books and lessons: Was the reading of books to come before the garnering of grain, which was our bread?

So it was my brother who meant most to me in my childhood. When we were alone together, fishing or wandering about the countryside, we exchanged secrets and dreams. We could talk of everything that we never said in words to anyone else.

Almost every Sunday we went to the Bjurbäck. We followed it through fields and water meadows where it had cut its channel. It flowed along through tangled fir woods, where the water moved black as ink under the heavy shadow of the trees and the air felt cool; we followed its windings through great boulders, where speckled burbot hung gaping beneath the stones, past old millraces where the water ran swift and steep, and over the grass of the meadow, where it glided slowly and calmly and widened into a river. The watercourse was our guide through unknown country; we could not lose our way. Here and there the Bjurbäck formed pools that seethed with fish; in the biggest of these pools eddies on the surface marked the movements of pike weighing several pounds.

In winter we clubbed the pike with axes under the ice of the pools; in summer we caught them in running nooses of fine wire, yellow-gleaming sieve wire. Sigfrid went ahead as scout and spied them out where they lay hidden at the edge of the stream under dandelion leaves and waterweed. In sunlight their scales flashed in one's eyes, but in shaded water or when the sun was overcast it was difficult to spot them.

As soon as we had snared a bunch of pike, we made camp in some glade by the stream, and rested. We lit a fire, cleaned a fish, grilled it on the embers, and ate it. We brought with us little boxes of raspberry and lemon powder which we dissolved in water, so that we had a cool, fizzy drink to go with the grilled fish. There was always a clearing nearby, where wild strawberries grew among the tree stumps; we ate as many of them as we could manage. Then, well-fed and content, we stayed in our camping place, stretched out on our backs and rested on the ground in the bright light of day. Above us sailed the clouds of a summer sky, light as the air itself, casting moving shadows over land and water. We lay humming and singing and felt as free as the wild creatures in the woods.

Sigfrid would talk about his future. He knew what he would do with his life. He would let no one and nothing spoil it for him. Soon he would be running it on his own. He was resolute and utterly assured. As assured, firm and resolute as only a youngster can be who is uncertain of himself, lost and perplexed in the face of the challenge: "Now it's up to you!"

Sigfrid had read a great deal; he read all the novels he could get hold of, and it was only from those books that he had learned anything of the world and its possibilities. He was now going to try them all. There were so many ways of using one's life, countless ones to choose from. He would like best of all to be an explorer and travel in countries where no white man had ever been before. And he would like to be a seaman or a balloonist too. But there were other things that attracted him: How would it be to become an actor, detective, lion tamer, caravan driver or conjuror in a circus? And the inventor's profession tempted him as well: He might become world-famous by inventing a perpetual-motion machine, which no one had yet been able to do. Or what about training as a diver and going down to see the depths of the ocean? No one knew what was hidden there. Or again, what would it be like to be a pasha in Turkey? How did a pasha behave in his harem, where he kept hundreds of beautiful women locked up? That might be fun—well worth trying.

Many kinds of occupation tempted Sigfrid, but there was one trade that he couldn't understand anyone's taking up: that of a butcher. We knew an old fellow, Slaughter Jonas, who came to us with his bunch of knives whenever some animal was to be killed. Sigfrid had a horror of this man: How could anyone take up killing as a trade? How could anyone serve Death, hire himself out to Death, make his living by taking life?

My brother had once said this decisively by Big Pool: He wanted nothing to do with death.

"What about you?" he said to me. "What do you want to be?"

Some years had yet to pass before I was old enough to have to make up my mind. But the thirteen-year-old knew exactly what he wanted to be, and I told Sigfrid: I wanted to be a learned man—a scholar. While I was studying Swedish history at school I had decided I would find out what life had been like for people who lived on earth before me. I would read everything that had been written about it. It would take a long time— many years, perhaps. I should have to learn several languages and read books as thick as the Bible. But life was long; I should have time enough.

Sigfrid wondered whether I realized what a scholar was—if I knew how long he had to study. I answered that I should find that out too, in time.

He said, "Always think to yourself, 'I'm here on earth just this once! I can never come back again.'"

Sigfrid said the same thing to himself: "Take care of your life! Take good care! Don't waste it. For this, now, is your time on earth."

So we lay resting under the bright clouds that glided over us and over the earth beneath us. We found our joy in experiences that we had never yet had—that were only waiting. We conjured forth endless possibilities that the world had to offer us. We dreamed them forth in the glade. One had only to help oneself: All this exists for you! What do you want? You've only to say. Here it all is in front of you!

Our campfire burned low as we exchanged dreams. We broke up new, dry branches from the wood and laid them on the embers. The fire flared up and blazed once more, and our cheeks glowed again with delight.

Sigfrid and I had everything here. The earth and all our time on it, our young bodies, our expectancy, our conviction—we possessed it all. We saw only a land of glory which it remained for us to travel through. We were a couple of young human beings, existing on earth just this once.

We lingered there for a long time.

The pools in the Bjurbäck had been named after their size or shape: Big Pool, Little Pool, Long Pool, Round Pool. But the name Crone's Pool originated with an old woman who had been drowned there when rinsing her washing. Biggest and deepest of them was Black Pool, which was reputed to be bottomless and whose waters were black, colored, it was said, by the leeches that swarmed in them, but they were really darkened by the deep shade of the fir woods. Round it was quagmire. The biggest pike in the whole river had their haunts here and were almost inaccessible to us. The surface was alive with water spiders, "tailors." When there were lots of tailors on a pool, there were plenty of fish as well. But when the surface was covered with the still, shimmering film which we called blue-silver, we knew that there was no life beneath it.

Blue-silver was like the stifling lid of a coffin; beneath it was only death. Such pools we called graves. We hurried past them, and never looked into their waters. Lifeless river pools were not for us.

During the dry summer of 1911 we caught multitudes of fish in the sunken, shallower pools—mostly small ones. We collected basketfuls of young pike. Father and Mother were pleased with this supplement to our usual fare. But Sigfrid said that catching pike in one's hands in a foot of water was not fishing. It was petty and easy—a sport for little boys. He was fully grown now, and big.

The water-carrying summer was hot, and hottest of all in July, the haymaking month. The drought stole much hay from us that year, but what remained was safely gathered in.

That summer I worked with the mowers for the first time. In earlier summers I had only turned the whetstone for the men when they sharpened their scythes. This was a little boy's job. Crank and bearings were well greased with big pieces of bacon rind and the wheel was easy to turn; it went round of its own impetus. But now Father had got a scythe ready for me; now I was a mower. The blade of my scythe was narrower than the other men's, and the haft was shorter, but the scythe was my own. I bore it proudly on my shoulder; I was to mow with the rest. I worked beside Sigfrid, and he showed me how to get at the grass between the stones with the point of my blade. To mow among stones without hitting them was a difficult craft. My brother taught me.

At five o'clock in the morning we went down to the meadow, for when the grass was soft with dew it was easiest to cut. As the sun rose higher and the grass dried and hardened, we needed keener and keener edges to our scythes. It was good to mow in the early morning in the shade; under the big oaks and aspens it was as cool as a cellar. Later in the day, with the heat, came thirst and sweat. Never before had we carried so much water to the mowers. They and the women who raked drank from great jars and pails. They kept calling for cool drinks, for the well water soon became tepid and no longer quenched their thirst.

But lovely were those cool mornings, full of the scent of dew-drenched flowers and grass and of the gentle rustle of the aspen leaves above us; and in the cool of the evening the air was easy to breathe.

Such should summer always be: not windy as spring mostly is, not rainy and chilly as autumn can be. This year it was a long, warm season that lasted from spring to fall.

The summer of 1911 was a gloriously long one—the last in which Sigfrid and I went fishing together by the Bjurbäck. I helped with the hay harvest for the first time, he for the last.

One Sunday in August we took our wire snares to Black Pool, the bottomless, about which Father and Mother had warned us. It was a day of bright sunshine. Sigfrid walked ahead, as always. We rocked over the bog; we were barefoot and our trousers were rolled up to the thighs. The shores of the pool were a quagmire, so soft that at every step we might fall through it up to our necks. We squelched along, the mud under our feet feeling like dough. When I walked over bogs I used to think of the girl who stepped on the loaf and with it sank into the underworld. To be smothered by mire was the most frightful death imaginable.

Quietly, quietly, we stole forward, so as not to scare the pike; but no matter how one tried, you could still hear that sloshing sound of the mud.

Suddenly Sigfrid stopped short, turned to me and with his hand to his mouth whispered, "Careful!" I halted instantly.

Now! Sigfrid had sighted something! And his wide eyes told me that he had spotted a big fish at the edge of the pool.

He took a step or two backward, cautiously and slowly, and on his long rod with the noose at the end he marked off a length with his hand—at least three feet. That big! A three-foot pike! I held my breath.

What happened next happened in ten seconds, and all that time I drew no breath.

Sigfrid set his running noose so wide that it could have encircled a balk of timber. Then he moved a step or two forward and lowered the shining wire into the water, moving it gently and warily. While I tried not to breathe, I followed my brother's movements. Now he had got the loop over the nose of the fish, now he was drawing the rod farther back along its body, now the wire must pass over the fins without touching them. The fisherman's hands gripped the rod, his lips were tight-pressed, his face pale; and the eyes that watched the fish down there in the water were wide. Softly the noose slipped round the prey in the depths—the prey I couldn't see.

Then it happened—and so quickly that I couldn't follow it! The white belly of a big fish flashed two feet above the surface—but only for an instant. After that

I saw nothing more. I just heard—heard a tremendous splash, as if a huge stone had whizzed down from heaven into the waters of the pool.

Wallow, wallow! It sounded muffled and heavy—heavy as a stone. Then all was quiet. Until I heard terrible noises from Sigfrid's mouth—coarse words, swear words.

My brother was cursing, and cursing in a way that would have appalled Father and Mother if they had heard him: "Hell and damnation!" And he called upon the Devil himself to carry him to perdition. I trembled with fright. What was the matter with Sigfrid? What had happened?

He came up to me with his rod, and I understood: there was no noose on it. The wire had broken, and the fish had taken the fisherman's tackle down into the depths.

There was still movement in the water, rings left by the Big One who had vanished with Sigfrid's snare.

For the rest of that day and for several days afterward he talked of nothing but the giant pike that he had lost in Black Pool. He had bought the strongest wire in the shop to make the noose with, but it was not strong enough; it had snapped. No further proof was needed of the size of that fish.

But was it a pike? Sigfrid was by no means sure. When he first spied it through the weeds he thought it was part of a tree trunk lying there rotting in the water. He had to look closer before he saw its head. And it was so broad across the back and so round of body—it didn't look like a pike. Now in the Bjurbäck we had never seen any fish but pike and burbot; yet who knew what others might lurk in the bottomless

Black Pool? The sheatfish, for instance: a gigantic fish that might weigh up to two hundred pounds or more.

He just had to solve the mystery. The very next day he went back alone to Black Pool. This time he had with him a noose of double sieve wire, two twisted strands twice as strong as the one he had lost. It would lift a balk of timber.

He came back empty-handed but in great excitement. He had seen the great fish again! It was easily recognized, for it bore a mark that was visible from a long way off—one that it had snatched from Sigfrid. The noose had caught in the dorsal fin! Round the fish, which was as thick as a tree trunk, the wire lay like a golden ring and flashed in the water. That was how he had spotted it. But the fish in the shining ring kept on the move, and Sigfrid could not reach it with his new snare. All the same he knew now that his quarry would not escape him. A fish bearing a glittering wire in its fin stood out from all other fish and was easily seen. It could not hide among the weeds, and he would land it without trouble.

But Sigfrid wanted to be alone when he caught the fish with the golden ring.

Summer was coming to an end. Dusk fell earlier, yet almost every evening he took his snare down to the stream. Each time he came back empty-handed, but just as eager and expectant; each time he had seen the fish swimming about in the depths in its gleaming noose.

He was now certain that it was no pike, though he couldn't say what sort of fish it was. It might be any of the various kinds that God had created and released into the waters that encircled the earth. And so this water creature that had stolen his pike snare turned into a thing of mystery. He had to hold this fish in his hands, he had to solve the riddle.

But my elder brother remained the fisherman without a catch; he kept coming home from the Bjurbäck with empty hands, and Father got irritated: What was the good of running down to the river all the time, when he couldn't catch so much as a minnow? This fishless fishing was a waste of time.

Sigfrid could have brought home a pitcherful of young pike and burbot if he had cared to. But he wasn't interested in that any longer. It was the fish with the golden ring that he wanted.

He saw it every time, swimming about down there among the rest like a wandering light. It moved like a lamp in those somber depths; and it seemed to preen itself, proud of its shining adornment, and opened its great wide jaws as if laughing. It mocked him when he lowered his snare into the water: "Come and get me!" And the fish struck out with his powerful tail, churned up great eddies in the water and was gone.

This could be nothing but magic. Sigfrid began to think that the fish he was trying to catch was one of the bewitched water creatures that old people talked about. In some waters, they declared, there were fish that nobody could catch—fish that weren't really there; they just glittered and gleamed and lured. They revealed themselves to the eyes of the fisherman, only to dazzle and fool him. Nobody could catch them in his hands because they belonged to another world than ours.

In time Sigfrid became convinced that in Black Pool there dwelt a fish that did not belong to this world— one that could appear and disappear at will. And that fish could live only in water that was bottomless.

102

But he would catch it; one day he would hold it in his hands.

Even the summer of 1911 came to an end and it was autumn. The waters of Black Pool rose with the rains and flooded the meadows, but the fish with the golden ring lived on in freedom in the depths of the pool.

Before the end of this year Sigfrid was to go forth into the world. But where? He had to find work to support himself. There was much talk at home that fall about Sigfrid's future: What should he do? Father and Mother thought there was not much choice if he would not take a job as farmhand or at one of the glassworks. He might go to America, where we had many relatives, but Mother was against that: All her brothers and sisters except for the eldest brother had gone over there and she had never seen them since. What was there left?

The village schoolmistress had told our parents that Sigfrid was gifted enough to study for the ministry, and he himself asked for nothing better than to go to college and learn something. But Father and Mother with their debt-laden small farm had trouble enough to scrape together a hundred kronor twice a year to pay the interest on it. They were too poor to keep a son at school in town, and must be content to have produced a son who *might have been* a pastor. They were rather proud of this: I heard Mother telling people what the schoolmistress had said.

But Sigfrid had read advertisements in the newspaper about a free school, the Regimental Volunteer Training School in Jönköping. Volunteers between the ages of eighteen and twenty-four were wanted. Young men of this age who signed on were guaranteed a good education. Those who enrolled for three years received free training that would qualify them for good positions in civil life. After those three years their future was assured.

Sigfrid read these Volunteer Training School advertisements aloud to me. Mightn't this free education be a good idea, since he couldn't afford to pay the fees at other schools? But then again there was rifle practice, and he hated the idea of handling weapons.

Now, looking back, I don't believe he would have applied if it had been left to him, but Father thought he should, and Uncle Nyström, Father's cousin, who was a corporal, intervened in Sigfrid's life that autumn. Nyström was a trusted man in our parish. Moreover he held the highest rank of corporal: Corporal First Class. He was our parish constable; he collected taxes and fines and helped the sheriff's officer to arrest people. He was held in respect. Father liked to mention his kinsman: "My cousin, the corporal first class."

Nyström also recruited volunteers for the Crown. He had enrolled his only son, who had had such quick promotion that he was now a sergeant with the regiment. Young Artur Nyström came home on leave and paraded himself about the district in his smart uniform, envied by the boys and admired by the girls. Artur had come up in the world, and this influenced us too; we were related to Sergeant Nyström. He called on us, dressed in his splendid furlough uniform. Artur was self-assured and superior; he had been out in the world. In front of him Sigfrid and I were silent and shy; we were just a couple of clumsy, ignorant hayseeds. Yet when we met Sergeant Nyström we realized what a poor boy could make of his life.

And when his father the corporal persuaded young-sters to go into service under the Crown, he held up his son as an example to all: "Look at *my* boy! Look at Artur! He started as a volunteer—he just signed on. And now he has a command. He's with the regiment —he handles the recruits. Artur is an N.C.O! A ser-geant!"

Mother said that Nyström was a miser who was feathering his own nest. She never really liked Father's cousin.

Uncle Nyström, as we called him, approached Sig-frid with the recruiting scheme: the Volunteer Train-ing School would suit him perfectly; it was the school for impecunious young men. It had suited his son Artur very well. And if after the three years Sigfrid was tired of the service, he could get a job in civilian life that entailed no drudgery. He could join the police, or be-come foreman or manager, or a railway clerk! His fu-ture was secure.

Father agreed with his cousin. Corporal First Class Nyström's advice carried more weight with him than anyone else's. This opportunity seemed made for his elder son, now that he was to go out into the world: free board, free lodging, free uniform and free school-ing under the Crown.

Sigfrid was lured by the good free schooling. But he asked Uncle Nyström about exercises and target prac-tice with the regiment. The answer was: "You'll have to go on maneuvers in a few years anyhow. No getting out of it. You've got to learn to handle weapons sometime."

True enough. But my brother hesitated for a long time: should he or shouldn't he? I later realized that he found it very difficult to decide. He never told me when he did. Perhaps because he knew what *I* wanted him to do: stay at home.

The decision came quite unexpectedly for me.

It was a Sunday just before Christmas. Uncle Nyström came to our place in the morning, and seemed to have been invited. Mother brought coffee and newly baked buns, and Father put the *brännvin* bottle on the table. And Corporal First Class Nyström behaved like a guest at a Christmas party: he was genial and talkative, he laughed and joked.

Sigfrid was to sit at the table too, but I was too young, so I crept into a corner and looked on. I had a premonition that something unusual was about to happen.

From his jacket pocket Uncle Nyström took out a large document which he spread out beside the coffee tray on the table. There were big stamps on the paper, and Father fingered it respectfully. I knew that when papers appear it means something important is afoot, but I didn't grasp what was going on at our table that day.

A human life was being determined. That Sunday was a day of destiny for my brother.

The document that lay spread out on the table was the recruiting form. Father poured *brännvin* into our guest's coffee cup and his own, and at Uncle Nyström's request Sigfrid too had half a glass poured into his. A soldier of the Crown must be able to carry strong drink, said the corporal. And Sigfrid was a big, tall fellow.

The corporal first class was not wearing his uniform with the yellow stripes on the sleeve, yet he had an air of authority and commanded respect. He was always the man who gave orders, and talked almost continuously. His hands twisted his big, fair mustache, winding and curling it and pulling at the points as if he wanted to drag them to the lobes of his ears. When he sipped his drink, the hairs dipped in the cup and got wet; then his tongue came out and sucked them dry.

My brother sat at the table too, but he said little. He answered Uncle Nyström's questions and Uncle wrote down the answers on the paper. It was like being examined in one's catechism. Whoever wanted to enlist had to write out his own application, the corporal said, and he would help Sigfrid to do this.

Sigfrid's height must also be entered in the contract. He had to stand upright against the door post and the corporal took out a tape measure and measured him: six feet four inches. A respectable height, not found every day among recruits of the Volunteer Training School.

Corporal First Class Nyström took hold of my brother's shoulders and felt them, and passed his hands over the muscles of his arms. "Fine! A fine volunteer! No one to touch you, boy!"

"Sigfrid hasn't ever been ill," said Father. "Never stayed in bed a single day."

"Splendid," said his cousin. "Nobody could be fitter than him. I think he's the finest recruit I've enrolled."

Mother did not sit at the table; she poured out coffee for the men and offered them cakes from the dish. She said nothing about the recruiting form, but looked a little anxious when the measuring and examination were going on, as if something dangerous were happening.

But everything about my brother was found to be fine and splendid, and he would be received with open arms by the regiment in Jönköping, said Uncle Nyström. The Medical Officer needed only to glance at him when he joined to see at once that here was plenty of health and strength.

The recruiting corporal wrote on, filling in the paper with words and figures, and Father talked eagerly and provided information when Sigfrid was uncertain.

It seemed to me that it was Father and Corporal Nyström who were doing all the recruiting, and that Sigfrid himself had hardly anything to say about it.

It was still not decided. Sigfrid's signature on the paper remained to be added. This last thing he had to do for himself. When the form was completely filled in, he must put his name to it and decide his own destiny.

Uncle Nyström dipped the pen in the inkpot and handed it to him. "Write your name, son! Better put all your baptismal names to be on the safe side."

"Sigfrid was only given two names at his christening," said Mother.

Sigfrid took the pen and held it motionless in his hand for a few moments. It was as if he were still considering. He glanced at Mother; she looked grave but said nothing. He glanced at Father, who looked impatient and said, "Go on, write! You've only got to put your name down."

And my brother pulled the big paper to him and wrote at the bottom: Axel Sigfrid Karlsson.

He had signed on for three years.

Uncle Nyström looked at the signature. "Writes well. Couldn't be better. He's got talent, this boy. He'll get on. Mark my words, he'll be lance corporal in a year." Soon Sigfrid would have authority, and would go round giving orders, "same as my Artur."

The recruiting corporal beamed with satisfaction. Father was content; he poured more *brännvin* into the coffee cups and thanked his cousin for his help. Mother said nothing; she had a wondering, inquiring look.

Afterward, when Corporal Nyström had gone and Sigfrid and I were alone, he said, "Now I shall get out into the world. That's why I signed. Because I don't want to be a home son any longer."

I had never seen him so cheerful.

Sigfrid left for the Regimental Volunteer Training School on New Year's Day, 1912. He returned home in the spring of that same year, in May. He had been discharged from the regiment. He had signed on for three years but was discharged after four months.

He had been ill at the school; that was all he told me. He still was not fit. He was up and about like the rest of us, and he worked with us, but at lighter jobs. When he exerted himself, he tired quickly and his back hurt. I soon became used to this, and knew that he tired easily.

He was unable to manage the mowing that summer, and I took his scythe. Sigfrid turned the whetstone for us haymakers when we sharpened our scythes. This was a boy's work; he sat on the ground and turned the crank. I was five years younger than he was, but I handled his scythe and he turned the stone for me when I sharpened the blade.

My brother had come back, but he was altered; he was thin, tired and sickly. He would get over it all right, he said; he must just eat plenty of milk dishes and other nourishing food. He would get fit again.

Not until long afterward did I know what he had lost to the regiment: all he possessed—his healthy young body.

A new summer came, but by now Sigfrid had nothing left.

I went with him to the Bjurbäck a few times; we went to Big Pool, where the largest fish were. Sigfrid took his pike snare with him, but he didn't fish any more. He was tired by the walk down to the stream, and sat down on a stone at the edge of the pool. He laid the snare across his knees, and did not walk round the water with it; he sat still on the stone, looking into the depths.

Sigfrid never caught the fish with the golden ring.

✟✟✟✟

WHEN I VISITED my home parish this summer, I went several times to the churchyard. It has all been redug since my brother was buried, and his grave has gone; it went many years ago. But I know where it used to be: under a young elm close beside the churchyard wall. The elm remains, though it is old now, and under it is a gravestone bearing a strange name: the name of a man born fifteen years before my brother and buried forty-two years after him.

Here, after nineteen years of life on earth, my brother's body disappeared, blended with other bodies, and became an ingredient of the soil. But when after fifty years I grieve over it, is it only for his sake? Isn't it also for my own?

I too failed to catch the fish with the golden ring.

I contented myself with other fish—smaller ones that I could trap in my hands. I caught little fish, good to eat but no fun to capture. I chose the easiest quarry, which required least effort. Now the fishing season is over, and all that remains for me is to contemplate my catch as it turned out to be.

Able now to survey events from a distance of fifty years, I distinguish those that were decisive in my brother's life. I can set them in their proper places, as causes and consequences. I can link together a chain of events that led to his last day.

111

Sigfrid lost his life just when he was to begin it. I know the dreams that filled his soul—all that he aspired to on earth and knew only in imagination. My brother's eagerness—his power to wish and desire—was boundless. He wanted to try many lives, and was granted not even one. He looked forward, he was convinced, he anticipated, he asked questions—but he received no other answer than nothingness.

I was allowed to keep my life. I still have it. How have I cared for it? I would work that out for myself if it were of any use. But if I had lived my life in any other way, I should be someone else.

Today I am an old man, but my brother Sigfrid is as young as ever: nineteen. He would have been nearly seventy today, but not for a moment can I picture him thus, as a grizzled, elderly man. For me he can never grow old. He is and remains the person I knew: a youth, tall, straight, strong and supple. I see a slim young body, a fine-skinned face under a broad forehead, big eyes under heavy brows, and thick fair hair. A lock or two falls over his forehead and he tosses it back with a jerk of his head. The few freckles on his nose almost disappear in winter, but in summer they come again. He smiles an embarrassed boy's smile which often takes the place of words when he is uncertain and doesn't know what to say. And when he smiles, one can see that a tooth is missing on the left side of his upper jaw. Sigfrid was and is nineteen.

Today we are an odd pair of brothers, he and I. In our youth he was five years older than I; now I am nearly forty-five years older than he. Today we are separated by a generation; he is the young man and I the old. And Sigfrid can never be old.

Father and Mother are dead; our brothers and sisters are dead. A few of our childhood friends are still alive, but they have long forgotten my brother, who left us at the beginning of the century. I am the only one who still remembers Sigfrid, the only one on earth who knows his life and retains his image. In me alone he lives on.

And when he rises again in my memory with his nineteen years, my own life shrinks to a tiny space of time. What is my life? Something that diminishes every time I draw a breath; an incident, a brief hiatus in something enduring; an episode in permanence, an intervening occurrence since which nothing has occurred. When I look back at Sigfrid's life I can see where I too stand: I live and breathe in a space between the era before me and the era after me. Here I spend the interval that passes with every breath I draw. Here I have my time on earth.

Half a century vanishes as if I had never seen it, never known it. What has become of all those years that have fled since we parted from each other, Sigfrid and I? What are those years when I compare them with the time during which we shall both be dead?

✝✝✝✝

SIGFRID RETURNED TO US in May, 1912; in July he died. During the intervening days he was very tired. I think I must have wondered at this sometimes, but I would certainly have been more anxious about him if I hadn't been dreaming of someone else at the time. Sigfrid had a secret from me, and I one from him. His secret concerned death, mine concerned life: I had fallen in love. I was experiencing my first love.

I was fourteen, the girl I loved was of my own age; and this was the only time in my life when I was and remained uninterruptedly happy in my love.

We were both in our last year at school, Katrin and I. In her body Katrin was already a young woman; she seemed fully grown and was almost as tall as I. My love for her gripped me and I surrendered to it helplessly. I think it started in the school playground, which was ringed round by tall balsam poplars. In memory my love blends indistinguishably with their fragrance. I see Katrin beneath the big trees that blossom before their leaves unfold and smell so strongly when in flower: a girl's body, lithe as a willow, weaving through the running games in the playground, from the sheer joy of movement; my beloved runs with swinging plaits under the green catkins.

The girl I loved has become the sight, hearing and scent memories of spring mornings in the playground. Katrin—a light-colored checked skirt clinging to the curve of her hips and fluttering about the long, girlish legs, the smell of a freshly starched cotton dress. Katrin—the grasses and flowers along the road to school, the stems of the cow parsley, the dandelion leaves and the newly kindled candles of coltsfoot by the roadside. She is a cooing laugh that is joy and pain, a caress and a whiplash. Katrin—the name rings like the ripple of the thaw in spring. My first love—she is the scent of poplar catkins on a morning in early spring.

I never heard any of my school companions say that Katrin was lovely; there was no need. Their treatment of her said it: the boys with their lingering eyes, the girls with their envy.

In my love I was like someone awakened abruptly in the early morning: bewildered, groping, afraid—above all afraid. How was I to behave so that no one found out . . . ? If she herself saw through me, what should I do? Could I survive it?

I came near giving myself away to Katrin herself one day when I saw her grieving. She was to be kept in to study her catechism, and when we left she remained sitting on her bench, weeping. I was seized with a desperate longing to share her punishment; I wanted to go and sit beside her on her bench. It would have been a happy thing to suffer with my beloved. But by doing that I would have betrayed my secret. And she must never know.

For she would certainly have made fun of me, laughed at me. And I could never have borne that teasing smile. Hers were the lips of a young woman: they were blood and flesh and red fullness, half open, mocking and maddening.

Katrin was the only child of a well-to-do farmer. He owned half a *mantal;* we had only a sixteenth. Her home was a place eight times the size of ours. She was the only child of a yeoman farmer; I was one of many born to a smallholder. I never dreamed of such a thing as marriage between us, any more than I should have thought of proposing to a daughter of Kaiser Wilhelm of Germany, the most powerful man in Europe at that time.

I never thought of Katrin as becoming my wife when I grew up. With her I could never be together in the way that married people were together. I could not imagine us lying in the same bed, she and I. I neither could nor wanted to do with her what a married man did with his wife.

Of sexual impulses I had only unpleasant experiences: regular nightly pollution linked with dreams that I was ashamed of when I woke. I dreamed that I was approaching the loins of big, plump women with powerful haunches and massive breasts. I don't remember that they had any faces; I didn't know them —except once, when I was afterward horrified: the woman had resembled Jenny, my big sister. The enjoyment of the climax was always strongly mingled with disgust. But from my purely sexual fantasies Katrin was excluded. She was in a high degree feminine: She had breasts, hips, arms and legs, she was flesh and blood, she was all that could trouble a boy. But about her I had only romantic dreams. She was an earthly girl, though I didn't want her to be.

What did I want of her? She was the object of the

newly awakened desires of the adolescent, which I repressed and denied.

How I desired her! It was worst during lessons, when she was near me. She sat on the girls' side in the classroom, but in the same row. Between us was a bench where two girls sat. For seven hours a day we were only two or three steps apart. So near my beloved did I sit, hour after hour, day after day, week after week, month after month, the whole of that last year of school! It was delight and torment.

I looked at her as often as I dared, but I feared to be caught doing it. I took my chance when she was looking in another direction. When her glance turned toward me I withdrew my own. She should not look into my eyes: they might betray me.

When Katrin sat on her bench bent over her exercise book, I could contemplate her face: her transparently clear skin, the glow of blood through it—a girl's skin with a gleam as of red cones on a young spruce. Katrin's face—the half-open, moist mouth and the fine down of her upper lip, soft as the fluff on a newly hatched chick. Her firm lips closed upon her pencil as she moistened the tip of it. The pencil in her hand could kiss her. Jealously I looked at this pencil which might go between my beloved's lips—that dead thing that she moistened with her mouth, that was permitted to kiss her living mouth.

And her eyes—what color were my love's eyes? I could never discover. I still don't know. The fourteen-year-old loved a girl to distraction and beyond all reason, but could never tell the color of her eyes. They altered: I saw them as dark green and light brown, as blue-black and pale green. They flashed angrily at one moment and shone mildly the next. Her gaze was mocking, her gaze was tender.

Both boys and girls said of Katrin that she was stuck-up and stupid. She was stuck-up because her father was rich, because of her pretty face, her smart frocks and shoes. And she was stupid: she had difficulty with her lessons. She did badly when there was questioning, and tried to avoid it; not until someone else had been given the question did she put her hand up, pretending to know the answer.

I kept my mouth shut when the others spoke ill of my love. If I had contradicted them and defended her, they might have guessed what was the matter with me. But in their behavior to Katrin the boys contradicted themselves. They showed off to her, they chose her in games before any of the other girls, although they called her stuck-up and stupid.

Boys and girls played "The Girl Goes in the Ring" on the playground:

The girl goes in the ring with the band of red gold,
To tie round her true love's arm . . .

The band of red gold was a handkerchief, which the girl tied round a boy's arm. Each time Katrin went into the ring my heart thumped: Would she come and tie it round mine? If she chose me, what would I do? It was just a game, but for me the game was deadly earnest: If Katrin came and gave me the handkerchief as she sang "To tie round her true love's arm," it would mean that she wanted me for her true love. And what would I do about that?

But my beloved never did tie the gold band round my arm in that game, and I never chose her in any other. I didn't because I so yearned to. I wanted to touch Katrin, to hold her. So I had to keep away. If I accidentally brushed against her it was like fire; I clenched my hands to prevent them from touching her.

I was furious with my hands for wanting to touch her; for not even to myself would I confess my innermost wish: to stroke Katrin, to pass my hand over her forehead, her cheek, her arm. I wanted to stroke her hair. I wanted to grasp her hand in mine and keep it there.

My hands were hot with lust to touch Katrin's body, and I clenched them hard to hold them back. A single caress with my hands, and I would be lost.

Once they almost hurled me to disaster. During a gymnastic class in the playground I happened to stand behind Katrin in the line, close up to her. Just in front of my eyes I saw the soft, downy hollow at the back of her neck, and my hands had her back and her thick plaits within reach. And her scent wafted to me: the scent of her skin, frock, hair—all that was Katrin rushed into my nostrils and forced itself into my brain. Sparks of sunlight burned in her hair and dazzled my eyes. I lost my head completely. I had no further control over my hands, and didn't know what they were doing. They seized her plaits and tugged them two or three times, hard.

I touched her, not gently and tenderly, but roughly. A sudden clumsy movement that hurt her. What had my hands done?

The next moment I wanted to sink through the gravel of the playground. Katrin spun round, her eyes blazing: "Leave me alone, you lout!"

She was seething with fury, and the saliva flew from the corners of her mouth. She would have gone on, but was checked by the commanding voice of the school-mistress: "Quiet in the ranks, Katrin!"

She obeyed and turned round again. I stared at the ground, played the innocent and felt a great relief: I had found an outlet for my desire to touch Katrin without betraying my love. I had not caressed her; I had hurt her. She must think I disliked her. And those nearest to us had heard her spitting at me and calling me a lout. This reassured me: my secret was now safe.

In the future I would take care never to come near enough to Katrin for my hands to reach her, for I could not trust them; they stretched out to my love of their own accord, without my willing it.

Yet the very next day all was changed between Katrin and me. Our first lesson was catechism, and before it started she came to me where I sat on my bench and asked me if I would please hear her recite her catechism lesson. The bit we had to prepare for that day was the most awful and horrible of the whole book, she said; she didn't understand the words, she couldn't learn all those long, complicated sentences by heart. Would I—? And she begged with eyes that looked into mine.

I was thunderstruck, and stammered a confused answer: of course. . . . I listened to her, and she thanked me. After that I realized that from my beloved anything could be expected. She was all that was changeable and unpredictable, in a girl's shape.

Something had happened when I tugged her hair; it was as if some tension between us had been released. I had made an approach to her and she had responded by asking me to hear her lesson.

This happened in the spring. In May we schoolchildren were sent out to plant trees to replace the ones that had been felled in the village copses. We escaped from our cramped classroom into the wide, wild woods, and we behaved like animals let out of their stalls to the first pasture of the year. For a few days we were released from lessons and hard benches; catechism and Bible history were cleansed from our minds. We were giddy with the freedom of the woods and the light of day over the countryside.

We made ourselves useful too: We sowed seeds of spruce and pine, hacking holes for them at the regular prescribed intervals. A young man in a green forester's coat and puttees, who was called a planter, directed the work. Our teacher was also with us, to keep order, but she paid more attention to the planter than to us, and liked to stay near him. In the woods she didn't bother about what we were doing.

During a midday break we played tag in a clearing. This was a popular child's game; one tagged another with a hand slap, and the tagged one tried to pass it on.

Katrin had been given the tag and had to pass it on to me. I set off running with all my might, and left her far behind. I wanted to show my love that I was swifter than she and that it was for me to decide when she should catch up with me.

I ran into the fringe of the woods before stopping and waiting for her. She might come now. I stood under a spruce fir, and Katrin came dashing after me, breathless and flushed with the effort. She came with such a rush that she ran into me, not having expected me to stop.

Suddenly we were standing close up against each other, out of sight of the others. She had run as fast as she could; she was gasping open-mouthed, and beads

of sweat glistened in the soft down of her upper lip. She
had caught up with me, but I had allowed her to. That
would annoy her. Now she would tag me.

But she didn't. She remained standing close to me,
and her hands were still.

I said, "Aren't you going to—?"

Then she caught hold of my hair with both hands,
hard. She was going to tug it, pay me back for what I
had done to her. I felt the breath from her mouth that
was so near mine; her tongue came out over her lip:
"No. But I'm going to—"

She had grasped my hair and pulled it. But all at
once her grasp slackened; her hands stopped pulling
and tugging. They had laid themselves on top of my
head, and there they lingered, warm and soft. She had
come so close to me that her breast was pressed against
my arm.

She had said, "But I'm going to—" What she was
going to do I never knew. The words ended with a
deep, cooing laugh, and her tongue hid again in her
mouth. But the hands on my head were still.

My love was touching me; I felt her breast yielding
against my arm, her mouth was open in front of mine
—and I didn't attempt to speak, not even to stammer.
For a few moments I was lost in dizziness; I believe I
was near fainting. I had once hit my head hard; I had
climbed up a birch and fallen, knocking myself out. I
knew what it was like to swoon, to float away, to feel
nothing and know nothing.

We stood thus perhaps for five or ten seconds, but I
experienced those seconds on the borders of unconsciousness: it was the most heavenly thing I had
ever known.

But Katrin took her hands from the top of my head,

passed them down over my forehead, and withdrew them. It was over.

"Tag!"

And she ran. She tagged me and ran from me. I stayed still under the tree for a minute or so before going on with the game—stood staring like an imbecile after the girl had run off again. What had she meant? What did she want of me? Her hands had caressed me—I had felt it so. Was it only through playfulness that she had touched me? And I had just stood there like a block of wood. What had happened to my hands, that I had always clenched so hard so that they shouldn't touch her? Why hadn't they flown out now to my love?

How many times I have wondered what would have happened if they had. What would have happened if I had drawn her to me? Would she have put her arms round my neck? Our mouths had been so close—would they have touched? Would Katrin's lips have opened to mine, as in school to her pencil?

I see two fourteen-year-olds standing in each other's arms under a spruce in the wood, trying to kiss—attempting a first caress, awkwardly, clumsily, shyly. And what would have happened next? No one knows. All I know is what would *not* have happened: We would not have taken what is known as innocence from each other. In the milieu we lived in and with the up-bringing we had had, we wouldn't have done that. And my feeling for Katrin shunned the physical experience; it could not have endured the realities of a sexual approach.

"But I'm going to—" Now I should never know what she wanted from me when she said those words. Was she drawn to me? Did she dream about me in the same way that I dreamed of her? But afterward she treated me as if nothing had happened. And I understood: Nothing *had* happened—for her. She wasn't serious about me.

But my love during the last year of my childhood was deadly serious. My love's hands once touched my head—and even now, fifty years later, I can relive the joy of those few heavenly seconds.

Never again was there any nearness between Katrin and me. My love for her fed on dreams, fancies and images. It had no bodily nourishment. But for that very reason I have it still undisturbed.

For me the thing was more serious than ever after our game the day we planted trees.

Katrin lived nearly three miles from our place, and after school ended I seldom saw her. That was the year we were confirmed, but boys and girls went to separate confirmation classes. For us, confirmation was the entrance examination that entitled us to the pleasures of youth. Once we had received our first communion, we were allowed to get out and enjoy ourselves; we went to dances.

Katrin was so precocious that she had learned to dance while still at school, and she stole out to dances long before she was confirmed. She did this without her parents' consent, and it was said that they were anxious about their disobedient daughter. They tried to lock her in on Saturday nights, but she sneaked out through the window. They couldn't keep her away from dancing. They were very God-fearing, and believed that she was possessed of an evil spirit—the spirit of the dance.

In summer the young people would gather on Saturday evenings at the dance floor in Bokhult, a lovely grove of big beeches a mile and a half from our farm. I knew that Katrin would be there, so I went to the grove myself without my parents' permission. I couldn't dance a step; I stood with the little boys and looked on. Every time a new tune struck up I saw Katrin on the floor. She danced every dance. She danced with boys who were much older than I; they may have been twenty or even more. They held Katrin in their arms with a firm, strong grip and natural assurance. And she followed them in the dance, willing, gay and smiling. Their hands were round her waist, and she yielded herself to their arms. She smiled at every boy; to every boy her eyes were radiant.

I watched how my beloved went from one lad's embrace into another's. Hardly had one partner's hands released her waist than another seized it. If only she had just put up with it, unmoved—but she liked it! She was delighted; she enjoyed it enormously. She wanted to feel the boys' hands at her waist. Her eyes shone, her mouth smiled, her cheeks bloomed. She sparkled with life in the dance; her feet glided over the boards, her hips moved gently as billows, her body swung as if borne up on wings. Like a bird she sped round in dance after dance, always partnered, always held in the hands of young men.

Between dances I moved away so that she shouldn't see me, but as soon as the music began again I came back. How could I stand there? How could I endure to see my beloved handled like that by other boys? Why didn't I leave? Katrin was as inaccessible to me as if she had been dancing on one of the stars in the sky.

When I went home after an evening's torment at the dance, I longed for death. I suffered—and I suffered with a grief that never passed. Other sorrows passed, but for this one there was no comfort. It could not end until life itself ended.

But I could not have borne the torment of my love alone for ever, and at last I confided in the one person I trusted—who would keep my secret as safely as I myself.

We sat on the bench under the big chestnut one warm summer's evening, Sigfrid and I. Mowing had begun, and with my scythe I had followed Father through the clover all that long, hot day. My brother had turned the whetstone for us, sitting on the ground. This was a couple of weeks before his death.

I confided my secret to Sigfrid; I told him what had happened to me at school this year: of my love for Katrin and of the agony it caused me. I told him how I felt when I saw her in the arms of other boys on the dance floor.

Other grown-up people would have laughed at the fourteen-year-old, but I knew that Sigfrid would feel for me.

He listened, silent and serious. He understood. He said, "Why haven't you spoken to the girl herself?"

"I'm afraid she'd laugh at me."

"You mean you daren't say anything?"

"No. Never."

"Then I don't see there's anything to be done."

"I'm afraid she'd tell the other boys and girls all about it, and then it would be all over the place. I should be a laughingstock."

"Maybe so. She's not to be trusted, perhaps."

Sigfrid understood; there was something that I

couldn't have endured. He said, "If you can't trust her, then there's nothing to be done."

"But I wanted to tell you about it. Makes me feel better." I was glad I had told him.

Sigfrid moved closer to me along the bench. "Now I'll tell you something too. Nobody else knows about it."

He paused, and then went on to say that he too loved a girl. He had loved her for years. He wouldn't tell me who she was; there was no need to mention her name. Anyway I didn't know her; she lived nearly six miles away. And it didn't matter whether I knew who she was or not. He had met her several times before he went to the Volunteer Training School, and they had written to each other while he was away. And she must have known what he felt for her, even though he had never actually put it into words.

But nothing more had happened between them than between Katrin and me.

I was astonished. I had always thought that Sigfrid didn't care about girls. My sisters used to joke with him about his shyness with them.

"Do you know whether the girl cares for you?" I asked.

"I think she did once. Now I don't know."

"Don't you meet any more?"

"Not since I came back. We haven't met at all since then."

"Why not?"

Sigfrid heaved a deep sigh. He looked away and for a moment seemed to be listening to something beyond the lilac bushes. "No, we don't see each other now."

"But why? Has she got married?"

"No."

"Has she got another boy?"

"Not that I know of."

"Then it can't be too late."

"Well, it is."

"Must it be?"

"Yes. We won't talk any more about it."

He said no more than that.

Sigfrid was silent; he plucked a leaf from the great chestnut that spread its dense foliage over our heads. The clover field next to the house lay new-mown, and the hay wafted its fragrance of drying flowers to our noses. Father and Mother had gone to bed and the mowers were resting. Our scythes hung on the plum tree over the grindstone, and the hay rakes were propped against the house wall. Men's and women's tools were resting.

It was the evening of the last weekday, the sixth of the days when men must work. Tomorrow was the seventh day, when men did not work. A boy in the next farm was playing on his accordion the waltz that boys were whistling and girls singing that summer. I listened to it and saw Katrin dancing away from me, farther and farther away: the girl who touched me and then ran—the girl I didn't reach out to when I might have.

But perhaps she would have run away anyhow.

Sigfrid had sat turned away from me for a time, as if busy with his thoughts. Now he came back. He said, "I wonder what it's like."

"What? What d'you mean?"

"Being with a girl."

"You mean . . ."

"To be with her really. I wonder."

His voice was low and I listened tensely, not to lose

128

a syllable. This was something we had never talked about.

"A boy and a girl—when they're closest of all to each other. What can it be like?"

"I know what you mean," I assured him eagerly.

"What can it feel like?"

"I don't know."

"No, you couldn't know either. But I've wondered."

And how often I had done the same!

"What do you think?"

How was I to answer that? What could I think? What did I know? What was I to say? I was silent.

"I try to imagine it. But when one hasn't—"

Sigfrid broke off, embarrassed. He sought for words and did not find them.

The youth of nineteen knew as little as the boy of fourteen. He had never caressed a girl's body, never touched her mouth with his. He wondered about the coming together; he had never even known the beginning of it. He was still at the questing stage: What could it be like?

He said, "I try to imagine it. But I'd like to *know. . . .*"

The evening of that haying day darkened over our farm. From the field beside us, where I had moved along with my scythe during the day, came the rich fragrance of drying clover hay. The day had been hard and the heat intense, but the evening was cool.

Two lads sat on a bench under a tree by a peasant cabin one evening in July, 1912. Then it was that I had my last confidential talk with Sigfrid, and he wanted to *know.*

✤✤✤✤

IT IS SEPTEMBER 1962, the middle of the vacation season, and the crowds on the sand at Pine Beach are at their densest. The Pacific Ocean spreads before them: a reviver of swarms of weary people. But the air is already cooler, and the morning mists rolling in from the sea grow ever thicker. Some days they linger on toward noon. Here in Pine Beach they don't feel raw and damp as they do farther up the coast; during my years in San Francisco I had a sore throat spring and autumn from the sea mists and the humidity of the air.

The other day I read in my morning paper about an earthquake in Bakersfield. No one was hurt, but there was a good deal of property damage. Last night I lay thinking about the thin, brittle crust of the earth which is our foothold, the security of our days.

This morning's post brought me a letter from Andrew, my younger son. He was named after his mother's father, Andrew W. Johnson, once my father-in-law. It was in his office that I worked many years as a prisoner of the real-estate business.

Andrew's letter is short and formal. He and his family are well. Business is good, and he has a lot to do. He says this in every letter; he has nothing else to talk about. I had asked after his mother, whom I never hear from. Andrew merely replies: "Mother in Gladstone is also very well." I learn no more about Esther than

130

that, and no greeting comes from my first wife through our son.

Andrew lives in Chicago, where he has a manufacturing business on Clark Street. He is successful in this. He always has a lot to do; his goal in life is that of the businessman, and a businessman is continually forced to increase his turnover or be crushed by his competitors.

My younger son has inherited his mother's talent for business, and looks down on me because I am bad at it. But my elder son—he was christened Albert after me—feels something like contempt for me because he thinks I am too good at it. So different are my sons. Their contrasting views on their father reveal much about themselves.

I have now wound up my last enterprise, the orange grove. I have sent off the last of the official letters, signed the last of the papers, settled the last contract. I have had my last business talk, presented my last demand and paid my last bill. Papers, figures, contracts, bank statements, checks, accounts—paper, paper, paper —have filled my life. That life is now over.

During these last years how eagerly I have looked forward to this day! I allowed business worries to rob me of sleep; snow fell on my orange crop; I could not get trucks to carry consignments when I needed them; I could not scrape together the wages for my pickers. When I bought the San Fernando property I never pictured the life of a fruit grower in the land of orange trees like this.

That last venture of mine lasted four years.

My resources, now that all has been settled, are much less than I had estimated. How long will they last?

I am sitting here, figuring. My body needs daily food and a bed at night. How much will it cost to keep it from hunger and cold? The rent of my little room at the Pacific—the cheapest in the hotel— including breakfast, is for a resident like myself $7 a day: $210 a month. Two other daily meals: at the cheapest eating places in Pine Beach I can get lunch and dinner for $4 all together, which is $120 a month. Board and lodging therefore come to $330 a month. Other necessary expenses—books, laundry, clothes, shoe mending, haircuts, shaving cream and other toilet things, newspapers at Mrs. Boles's drugstore, bus fares (I occasionally go into Los Angeles) and unexpected expenses—what will they amount to? I have no office expenses now; just postage stamps. And I write few letters these days: just to my two sons and to Annie, my second ex-wife. But for sundries I shall have to reckon at least $3 a day or about $100 a month. So I shall need about $430 a month if I'm to stay on at the Pacific.

I shall be able to stay only a short time in my hotel room between the town and the ocean.

Today I lunched at Cabrillo's MEXICAN FOOD. I have discovered that grilled lamb chops are 25 cents cheaper here than at other small restaurants in Pine Beach. And he amuses me, this joker Cabrillo, who publicizes his restaurant by making himself out to be a descendant of the Columbus of California. He gives his customers the full treatment with this piece of romance.

Today I asked him to supplement my knowledge of California history. The name California first appears in print in the novel *Las Sergas de Esplandián*, by the Spaniard Ordóñez de Montalvo. This book recounts the adventures of the son of Amadís de Gaula, who became the model for *Don Quijote,* and described California as a supernally marvelous island situated to the right-hand side of India, quite near the borders of Paradise. This island was a Garden of Eden. The inhabitants kept tame bears and lions as domestic and riding animals, and all their weapons were made of gold. They knew no other metal. Perhaps the designation Golden State did not originate with the gold rush of a hundred years ago. Might it be three centuries older?

Cabrillo instructed me, speaking as schoolmaster to pupil. It was like this: While under the Spanish Crown California was a blessed land—almost a Garden of Eden. And during the first half of the nineteenth century, when it belonged to Mexico, it could certainly be compared to the earthly paradise. Then the Americans came and stole it from Mexico, and now after a century of American rule the Golden State had been so transformed that it resembled hell.

I refused to accept this story. I did not believe that California had ever been a paradise, even during the unknown, unrecorded days before the discovery of America. The innocent state of nature of the original inhabitants, the Indians, was not happy by our standards, and would never tempt us to live the life of the ancient Indian tribes. Their food, for instance, consisted of unpleasant animals which they ate raw: skunks, rats, insects, lizards, snakes and other reptiles. Grasshoppers and beetles were considered great delicacies.

"How would you feel about eating insects and snakes raw, Mr. Cabrillo?"

The Mexican bared his shining teeth. The Indians'

diet was primitive, certainly, but the Spaniards introduced civilized eating habits into the country. It was the people of his own race who brought culture to California.

"I suppose you've never heard of Father Serra, who planted the Cross on this coast?"

I replied that of course I knew about Father Serra, the St. Francis of the New World. When he arrived in California he was too ill to walk, and was carried ashore on a litter. But he founded nineteen religious houses here, and must have been a most able man in his own line.

"Father Serra was one of the greatest men in the history of the world," Cabrillo declared. "He started the baptism of Indians and saved countless souls from eternal damnation. Who could perform a greater work?"

The proprietor of MEXICAN FOOD is an ardent Catholic and goes regularly to Mass.

"Father Serra also tried to abolish the frightful custom of polygamy among the Indians. You know about that too, of course, Mr. Cabrillo?"

"Why, of course! Why shouldn't I?"

But his voice wavered, and I pursued the matter: What did he think of the sexual customs of the original inhabitants? Indian women were treated like cattle; they were bought and sold like any other goods. As soon as a man wearied of one wife he got rid of her and bought another. The number of wives depended solely on a man's means. Rich old men bought beautiful young women and had a monopoly of them, while poor young men couldn't afford even one wife.

The eyes of Cabrillo, the bachelor, flashed. He is reputed to be a great consumer of women, and there

134

have been many rumors about his onslaughts upon the female staff of MEXICAN FOOD.

He passed his hand slowly over his thick, well-tended hair. Polygamy, said he, was a human phenomenon which has always interested him—in principle, that is. For virile men it provides a fundamental solution to the problem, since their sexual needs cannot be satisfied by one woman only. In many cases it might be the only solution.

From his tone I received the impression that he had had extensive experience of cases when polygamy provided the only solution.

"Of course I'm speaking only of really strong and virile men," he added.

"But in the case we're discussing it was the feeble old men who bought all the women!"

His teeth flashed again, and his smile broadened. "Yes, indeed. And yet you still say, Mr. Carlson, that in California there was never a state of happiness?"

Juan Rodríguez Cabrillo was absolutely right: For elderly male aboriginals California must have been Paradise indeed.

🌳

Daily life in Pine Beach is shaped by the ocean. The inhabitants carry the roar of it in their ears. For them the word Ocean has an enormous capital letter. When they say "the Ocean" one knows that they are not alluding to the Atlantic or Indian Oceans. For the people of Pine Beach there is no other ocean than their own, rolling to their very doors. They have taken the word and given it to streets, buildings, gardens: Ocean Avenue, Ocean House, Ocean Park.

Today I was up early and set off on my walk while the tide was out. As I returned over the dunes, it turned and began to come in. On approaching the hotel I met a man walking alone; he kept near to the wall of sand that the breakers had built: a tall figure with bushy hair and long beard, dressed in a full, mantlelike coat, blue-green as the sea. He walked barefoot over the sand, and the skirts of his coat flapped like the wings of birds round his thin, naked legs.

At his post at the Surf-San Pedro intersection Jesus Jensen is a singular, distinctive figure. But out here in the dawn, on the deserted beach, with sea, rocks and dark cypresses as his background, he is one with his surroundings. Here he resembles the originator of Christianity, walking along the shores of the Lake of Gennesaret.

We were two early-morning walkers. We halted beneath a giant cypress with massive, crooked, drooping boughs, and talked together.

The sea had turned and was coming nearer and nearer to us. With a soft murmuring the water rolled up the shore. The ocean was drawing calm breaths after the night, as if in lingering dreams.

Jesus Jensen said that he had never seen me in a car. Didn't I have a car? No, I told him; I had just sold one and wasn't going to buy another.

"Very wise of you! I tell motorists every day: Stop driving! Scrap your cars! Stop the Death Machine!"

"Death Machine?"

"Yes! I want to save people! I want to save the forty thousand people who would otherwise be killed next year!"

Jesus Jensen clutched me by the collar of my jacket, hard, as if this might help me to understand.

Statistics for the past ten years, he said, showed that an average of forty thousand people in the United States lost their lives in car accidents every year. The automobile killed more than one hundred people every day. Every day over one hundred mangled, crushed, dismembered human bodies were left lying on our roads. Every hour four people were slaughtered. Every quarter of an hour the Death Machine devoured a living creature. Imagine: Every quarter of an hour—now, at this moment, during this day, and tomorrow, the day after, the whole week, next week, next month and so on through the year, and then next year and the year after! Forty thousand lives to feed the Death Machine! The population of a medium-sized American town murdered in a single year!

For Jesus Jensen the national highways were a battlefield, covered with the dead. Bodies were cleared away, only to be replaced by others. These hundred corpses lay there every day. Moving them simply added to traffic.

The hair of the speaker fluttered in the wind from the Pacific Ocean; he turned to face the sea and raised his voice: "Which does a man choose, life or the internal-combustion engine? Which is more valuable? Which can he best do without? Can all the automobiles in the world replace a single living human being? Can all the cars in the world restore a dead man to his widow? Can they bring back a dead child to its parents? How do you choose: to die—or to live on in a world without automobiles? Answer me! Which do you choose: to sacrifice yourself or your car?"

The wind carries away the speaker's words. The sea draws near to us and takes back the shore, flood tide comes ever closer to our feet as we stand under the cypress. Advancing waves wipe out my footprints, fill up the hollows in the sand. In a moment no eye will detect the steps I have just taken.

"Answer me!"

And I answered, saying to Jesus Jensen that I could well imagine living my life in a world without motor traffic; that I had no goal to be reached within a certain average mileage per hour. But I also said, "Fifty million people drive cars in the United States. Not one of them seriously expects to become one of the forty thousand smashed-up corpses lying on the roads each year. So they keep on driving. Just like soldiers summoned to war, each of *them* believes in his heart that he'll survive. That's how wars are still possible."

The Dane is not listening. He has worked himself up; he has planned a great project, which he is going to put before the public in press, radio and television. The bodies of all those killed in traffic accidents should be preserved and assembled somewhere in the California desert. Death Valley would be an appropriate place.

Jesus Jensen is to propose that the forty thousand victims of the Death Machine, the internal-combustion engine, should be heaped up in the desert in one great mound, piled one upon the other. A building of bodies, a pyramid of corpses, which would increase by forty thousand every year. It would soon soar hundreds upon hundreds of feet into the air—higher than any pyramid of Egypt. It should then be shown to every car owner in the United States. They would have to come and behold this structure—this steeple of the dead in the desert. It should be made compulsory: Everyone must visit the Road-Death Valley in California. And when they had beheld the work of the Death Machine and seen the pyramid of corpses reaching to the sky, they would return home and send their vehicles to the automobile graveyard.

My fellow Scandinavian asked my opinion of the plan. "Effective, don't you think?"

"Effective, certainly, if it could be carried out."

Jesus Jensen's eyes look piercingly into mine. "You don't think it could be done?"

"Frankly, no."

"You'll see! I'll do it! I've staked my life on it! The great task of my life is this: Stop driving!"

The Pacific Ocean comes nearer to us; the murmur of the water grows louder with the tide's advance and rises to a roar from the depths. From Surf Street come sporadic noises: traffic squeals and rumbles. Soon it will be morning; the Pine Beach traffic is getting under way, and before long the voice of the town will drown that of the ocean.

Jesus Jensen says, "We've been standing here for a quarter of an hour. During that time one person has been fed to the Death Machine. Perhaps a youngster —an eighteen-year-old who has just begun life."

I tell Jesus Jensen that his idea of building a pyramid of traffic-accident corpses in the California desert would be impossible to carry out in our modern society.

Have I hurt him by my lack of faith in his great project?

But all he says is "You know the nickname they've given me in Pine Beach?"

I nod. His beard and mustache are cleft in two, revealing a mouth and broad powerful teeth in the upper jaw.

"Jesus Jensen! Yes! And I know of course that in Pine Beach I'm considered a freak!"

With that he holds out his hand, grips mine firmly,

says good morning and goes on his way along the beach with long, swift strides. His bare feet sink into the sand; his coat flaps about his thin bare legs like a winged bird. But after him the tide runs up and washes away his footprints.

I have met the town idiot, who declares that all the automobiles in the world are of less value than a single human life.

I have met the most harmless inhabitant of Pine Beach: a wise man.

❦

One day at a time goes by; another day has passed. I stretch out in my bed and wait for sleep.

". . . replace a single living human being . . . perhaps a youngster . . ." This one and only time on earth!

The heavy rumble of the sea returns to my ears, blending there with a lighter, brighter sound: the ripple of running water, of a stream. Gently I breathe in and listen. Am I really hearing it? Can I hear that stream from the other side of the world? My hearing has become dulled now, but is renewed and sharpened at night. I hear new, peculiar sounds.

The sounds of two waters blend into one in my ears tonight; one roars outside these walls; the other ripples six thousand miles away.

I again find the place, the meeting place, the resting place. Our campfire has died down, but I gather brushwood and dry branches and revive it. It blazes up and burns as before, and as before I stretch out on my back on the mossy ground.

"You've been away a long time."

I answer him, "Not long. Now I've come back."

☙☙☙☙

IN 1911 WE HAD THE DRY SUMMER; 1912 was the year
with the wet late summer and autumn. June and July
were sunny, but with August the rain set in. During
August and September it rained nearly every day; not
only rained but poured. In the fields the reaped grain
hung drenched on the racks; it sprouted in the ear and
was ruined. The yield of 1912 was the richest we had
ever had on the farm, but little of it was garnered.
Much of the rye, our bread, was fit only for pig food,
and the violent rains beat holes in the old turf roof of
our cabin. We had to get up at night and put tubs and
buckets under the holes, for the water dripped and
trickled into our beds. During one nocturnal rainstorm
we collected all the vessels in the house, from the biggest copper pan to the smallest milk jug.

The wet autumn gave us much hard work with the
crops. Father was in the fields from dawn till dusk; he
allowed himself no rest while daylight lasted, and he
could do anything in the open. He moved mostly at a
jog trot. When he came in to supper with us he said
little. Father had grown taciturn. I guessed why.

The Sunday of Sigfrid's burial I had seen him weep
as the coffin was lifted onto the cart. After the funeral I
seldom heard him mention my brother's name. He and
Mother sometimes talked about Sigfrid, I knew, but

when I came within hearing they stopped. I wondered why.

Mother's eyes had changed. They had somehow crept inward; they had shrunk. Perhaps it was because she rubbed them so often; they had begun to itch in a funny way, she said. But other things set their mark in people's eyes.

The red on our cabin had flaked off and faded, and we had intended to repaint that summer. We had already bought the paint, but nothing came of it. Mother said, "I don't want to see the place bright red any more."

She had her way. Father said we could put it off till another year. There was no hurry; it could stay as it was until another summer.

Our house was a house of mourning; red was joy and black was sorrow. But our cabin was neither the one nor the other; its walls were gray. And I didn't care whether we painted it this year or next. What we did have to do was to put a new turf roof on it, said Father.

The Bjurbäck rose with the great rains, the water meadows were flooded into lakes. I went fishing alone that autumn. Often it seemed to me that Sigfrid was there too, walking ahead of me with his snare fixed to the rod, and peering for pike among the weeds and lily pads. Walking alone there, I often talked to him and he answered. I was in touch with my brother by the stream.

I had been utterly unprepared for his death. Nobody had told me that he was seriously ill. And now I asked Mother to explain how Sigfrid came to die so suddenly.

"He got something wrong with his kidneys when he was away," said Mother. "Albumen in his urine. Blood too, sometimes. I think Sigfrid's kidneys were ruined."

This was what Father and Mother knew about his illness: He had sickened after an exercise at the Volunteer Training School. When he came home that spring he brought a paper with him from the Medical Officer, which he showed them. The name of the illness was written on the paper; it was in Latin, so it meant little to them. But there was something about disease or damage in the kidneys. Mother said that she and Father had only looked at the paper once; then Sigfrid threw it in the fire and burned it up. It was the doctor's certificate to show why he had been discharged from the regiment, he said. Now he was home again, he didn't need the paper any more, so he threw it in the fire.

"But it was something incurable he had," said Mother. "Sigfrid was deadly ill—that's why they sent him home. Unfit for service."

"Did *he* know that?" I asked. "That it was deadly?"

"He thought so, o' course. Seeing as how they discharged him."

"How long had he known?"

"Since the spring. Since he came home again."

"And you and Father knew too?"

"He told us, but not anybody else. He didn't want anybody else to know."

"Sigfrid never said anything about it to me. Never once."

"He didn't want you to know."

I stared at Mother; the heart in my breast stopped beating.

"Did Sigfrid say that?"

"Yes, he did. Many a time."

"So that's why!"

"Yes. And why should we ha' said anything?"

So my discoveries began. Incidents that I had puzzled over during the summer began to clarify; things my brother had said and done now acquired another meaning. I thought back to our summer after his return in the spring, and it was transformed: "He didn't want you to know."

Sigfrid had told me that his back hurt. That hadn't worried me; nobody died of a pain in the back. Father, too, often complained of a bad backache, and no one could be healthier than he was. But once at the beginning of summer, when we were working alone together, I began to feel anxious about Sigfrid.

He wanted to help with all the jobs on the farm, although he had said he wasn't fit. Father used to say, "You don't have to do more than you've strength for. Take a rest when you're tired." One morning he sent us both down to sharpen fence stakes in the copse. We each took an ax and went to a clearing where all the juniper bushes had been cut down. The juniper stakes were stacked together in a great pile, to be stripped and hewn into points at the thick end, before being driven into the ground to make a fence.

After working for a few minutes Sigfrid dropped his ax and sat down on a stone, clutching with both hands at the small of his back.

"Blast it! Get such a wicked pain here when I chop."

He had sharpened only two stakes and begun on a third when he sat down to rest. He pinched his lips together and his face was twitching.

He picked up a shaving, chewed it and muttered, "Aren't I even fit for this? This kid's job?"

Sharpening stakes required no effort; little boys could manage it. But my brother couldn't. He who until lately had been so sturdy, so strong. How Corporal Nyström had praised the new volunteer when he enrolled!

I asked him what was really the matter, and he replied that it was simply his old backache. It came when he bent over. It would soon pass off. If he sat and rested a bit, it would go.

I said I thought he could rest for a while; there wasn't all that hurry for these old stakes. "Take five minutes off," I said.

We had to bend to chop at the stakes, and it was that position that made Sigfrid's back ache. "Hurts when I bend down."

After a few minutes he slowly straightened his back, took his ax in his right hand and the juniper stake in his left and began again.

He worked silently. In a little while he had to sit down again. Letting his ax fall, he said, "Soon as I start chopping, something chops me here in the back. What d'you make of that?"

Father had given us this job to do. We were to sharpen all the stakes in the stack before going home to dinner. And Sigfrid insisted that we should finish it.

He hacked, sat down, then took up his ax again: "If only I didn't have to bend over. If I didn't have to stand crooked."

We finished all the stakes; but when we walked back through the copse, Sigfrid was very tired. He walked slowly, and once or twice he sat down by the wayside and held his back: It hurt, but it would pass off, he said. He would just have to rest a bit.

And only now after his death did I learn that he knew he had been discharged and sent home from the school as incurably sick. He had come back to us with

145

death in his body. He knew this, but hid it from his brother; nobody was to tell me. During the time that was left to us I was not to dream that he was soon to die. He had spared me this knowledge—and it hit me now, when he was no longer there.

The living man had been close to me; the dead one came even closer.

My elder brother, Sigfrid, had set forth into life— and it cost him his life. Something must have happened to him during the four months he had been away with the regiment. What could it have been? He was fit and strong when he went to the Volunteer Training School; he had hired out his healthy young body to the forces of the Crown, and never got it back. What had happened? How was it that death entered into him?

I was to know in the end, but not for a long time. A very long time.

IN THE AUTUMN OF 1912 I continued to question Mother about Sigfrid's illness, but she merely said that she had told me all that she and Father knew about it. I wondered why they hadn't sent for a doctor, as he was so very sick.

"He said it was no good getting a doctor, besides the army doctor, 'cause he was incurable."

But, I said, that Friday evening when Sigfrid went to bed earlier than the rest of us, and didn't wake up next morning—they ought to have sent for a doctor then.

"We knew there was nothing to be done," said Mother. "And when he lost his senses we knew he'd soon be gone."

At that time no doctor had ever entered the house, and I was told that no doctor could have saved Sigfrid. Now I heard that Uncle Johannes had stayed with us that Saturday night, while I slept. They had sent for him instead of for a doctor.

Mother's voice was somber when she added, "Afterward I was sorry we didn't send for the pastor."

"Could the pastor have cured him?"

"You see, I keep thinking—did Sigfrid get away safe?"

Then it came—she blurted it out as if against her

will: "I can't help thinking . . . did he get away safe from here?"

Sigfrid was gone, but Mother was still anxious about him. She was afraid that he had died unsaved and gone to hell.

I was outraged on his behalf: What had Sigfrid ever done in his life that he should be punished with everlasting fire?

Mother told me that she had never feared for my other brothers, who died very young. They were with God. They had not had time to commit any sin. But Sigfrid was fully grown when he left us. He was nineteen. He had had time to sin. He needed forgiveness for his sins. But now she didn't know: Did he find forgiveness before he died?

I couldn't believe that he had done anything that needed forgiveness.

And it seemed to me that Mother herself was now sinning against Sigfrid; she did him a great injustice when she spoke this way.

I wanted her to stop worrying about my brother; but what could I do? What was I to say? Sigfrid had ceased to believe in hell, and he had comforted me when other people tried to scare me with it. He didn't believe in any Our Father in Heaven who rewarded the good and punished the wicked. But if I had told her this I would have horrified her, and she would have been certain that he was among the damned in hell.

I couldn't console my mother with words that would have upset her more than ever.

"Sigfrid was good and obedient as a child," Mother said. "He almost always did what he was told."

Then I reminded my mother of the promise in the

catechism: that he who honored and obeyed his parents should live long upon the earth. Sigfrid had kept this fourth commandment, but he hadn't been allowed to live long. He had been obedient, but lived only nineteen years. God had broken the promise in that commandment.

Mother was stern in her rebuke: "It's not for you to meddle in God's purposes, boy!"

But she regretted not having sent for the pastor. They ought to have done that on Friday evening, before Sigfrid lost consciousness. The pastor could have administered the Sacrament and talked to him of Jesus, the mediator between God and all sinners. On Sunday morning when he didn't wake it was too late; by then he knew nothing of anything about him, and most likely the pastor would just have said a prayer by his bed. But on Friday night . . .

There had been so much to do just at that time. They were bringing in the last of the hay while the dry weather lasted. They had thought too much of earthly things. Afterward she and Father had reproached themselves because Sigfrid had not taken communion. It was a piece of negligence for which God might call them to account.

"I asked Sigfrid once if he ever thought about it," Mother said. "If he ever thought about his end."

"Did you ask him if he was ready to die, then, Mother?"

"Yes, I did. We were sitting on the settle in the kitchen talking together. And then I asked him. He just stared at me—stared hard. But he didn't say anything. He never answered. He got up and went out. I never did find out."

I thought I understood why he got up and went out.

149

"So I never knew whether he ever thought about it in his mind. But we must hope for the best. We just have to trust in God's grace and mercy."

Mother wondered what happened to Sigfrid after he left us. I wanted to know what had happened to him before, while he was still alive, during those four months when he was away from home.

I got out the letters he had written to me from the Volunteer Training School—I still have them—and read them through again. Each one was a full page or more. But all they told me in a few short sentences was about his daily life in military service: "Yesterday we went on a long route march, and we were up on a high hill where we could see 25 miles all round. . . . It was funny. . . . Today we had church parade, and there was a new pastor who preached. . . . The colonel came today, too, so it was all the flags up and the band playing. It plays quite often. We volunteers at the school are soon going to be moved and posted to our different companies. . . . I have met quite a few I know from home among the new recruits . . . it's nice to meet people one knows. . . . The food is getting better. I am fit and well. . . ."

Each letter was signed "Your uniformed and numbered brother Sigfrid."

I wanted to know how his body got damaged while he was with the regiment. Someone or something must have been to blame. But in his letters he never said a word of anything unpleasant in the service. He simply wrote that he was fit and well. In every letter he asked for news from home. He was away and we wanted to know how he was getting on, but he wrote chiefly about us at home.

But perhaps he had left something that would say more than his letters did? I remembered his trunk. What was in that?

When Sigfrid went to the Volunteer Training School the village carpenter had made him a little yellow-painted wooden trunk. In this he kept his belongings. He had brought it back with him, and now it was stowed away in the loft. Nobody had bothered about it since his death.

I hadn't been up to the loft since Sigfrid had lain up there on the plank of the bench-chest. I went now to look in his box. It was unlocked; I opened it and began to go through it. I found books and papers, letters and notebooks from the school, and it wasn't long before I came upon a book in which I made discoveries about my brother.

It was a small book with a blue cover and a yellow leather spine: Sigfrid's regimental textbook: *The Infantryman's Manual*. He had once shown it to me and told me that it was the most important book he had had in the service: it was the soldier's bible. The conscripts who were forced to go on exercise had christened it the Bumpkin Bible: It was fit for the stupid volunteers who had joined up of their own free will and were therefore called country bumpkins. I was indignant. Fancy calling Sigfrid, the cleverest boy in his school, a country bumpkin!

I shut the lid of the trunk and sat down in the loft to read the blue-and-yellow book. Inside the cover Sigfrid had written his name and number.

At school he had "passed with distinction" in handwriting; and how well I recognized those big, firmly rounded characters:

This book belongs to Volunteer No. 112,
8th Company, the Royal Kalmar Regiment
Axel Sigfrid Karlsson.

But beneath his name and number he had written something else. He had added a line—later, for it was written in different ink. Blacker ink:

The fool who sold his soul to the Devil.

So then I knew what my brother had done that Sunday last year, when hesitantly he set his name to the recruiting form. He had written and spoken of it himself; he had written it down with his own hand in the soldier's bible. It was here for all to read inside the cover of *The Infantryman's Manual.*

This little blue-and-yellow book had ruled my brother's life. He had said that this was his most important book at the Volunteer Training School. His bible.

On the next page I read: *His Majesty has been graciously pleased to approve this revised version of* The Infantryman's Manual, *at the Palace of Stockholm, 2nd May 1900.* The Secretary of State for War had signed his name below, in the textbook which His Majesty had been graciously pleased to approve, and in accordance with which Volunteer No. 112 Karlsson was to conduct his life.

I went through the soldier's bible from cover to cover, turning the pages with eager fingers. I did not read the printed text, but skipped it all; I looked for handwritten passages in my brother's writing. He had made entries on many pages. He had written in the margins, beside the print, or in spaces between sections

152

of it. My dead brother was talking to me. He was talking about himself—and here I found what I had been looking for: Volunteer Sigfrid Karlsson, 8th Company, the Royal Kalmar Regiment.

He came to me in his own handwriting, and I needed to look no farther than the chapter on small arms:

The bayonet is fixed to the rifle to enable this to be used as a stabbing weapon. It consists of blade and hilt.

Beside this three sentences were written:

"The bayonet is like the knife that Slaughter Jonas drives into the throats of animals. But Jonas stuns them first—I'm learning to stick a knife into people without stunning them.

"I'd have done better to stay at home and bind myself apprentice to Slaughter Jonas."

At many places in the soldier's bible Sigfrid wrote about the implements of death that he was handling every day. He gave a clear indication of his service life: "According to the commandments in the Bumpkin Bible my incessant task must be to prepare myself fully for the profession of war. I am to learn to bring about the destruction of other people."

Two words recurred, two words, written variously in small letters and capitals, with and without hyphen, spaced and unspaced: Three years. THREE YEARS. T-h-r-e-e y-e-a-r-s. T H R E E Y E A R S. At the end of the book years were turned into days, with a subtraction sum: "1,095 for Volunteer Karlsson. 63 days have passed, leaving 1,032. Only!"

When I had gone through *The Infantryman's Manual* from cover to cover, I knew about Sigfrid's life during his military service.

On the very last page of the book there was no printed text, but a short handwritten note:

"15 May. Going home today. But why must I die when I want so much to live?"

The book with the blue binding and the yellow spine was a message to me from him who was no longer there. I took good care of it, and still have it. *The Infantryman's Manual* is the most precious memento of Sigfrid that I possess.

His question on the last page has accompanied me through the countries and wanderings of fifty years.

I felt that my brother had made the notes in this book on purpose for me, to be read when he had gone. He never meant anyone else to see them, for no one else would really have understood. Mother, for instance! Mother, who was so much afraid that he had gone to hell—suppose she had read in his own words that he had sold his soul to the Devil!

Now I had to safeguard the message he had left to me, so that no one else could get at it. What would be a safe hiding place? In the end I hid the soldier's bible in the loft, where the yellow trunk was in which I had found it. I shoved the little book between the turf and the birch bark of the roof. There it would be safe, and nobody would find it. Now and again I looked to make sure that it was still there. Now and again I still take out my brother's *Infantryman's Manual,* to read not the printed text but the handwritten notes.

There I find Sigfrid and the implements of death. His comparison of the bayonet that he was to learn to fight with and Slaughter Jonas's knife recalled an incident to my memory. It happened when I was quite small, the year we moved to the farm.

✣

Our father had the manual skill common to all countrymen in my childhood. He could handle hammer and plane, saw and chisel. He made much of his gear himself, and mended it when it broke. But there was one trade that he had never learned: that of the butcher. He hired a man for that job. When any beast of his was to be killed, he sent for Slaughter Jonas.

Jonas was a traveling slaughterer; he went his rounds about the countryside, stabbing and skinning animals for the farmers. When slaughtering day came, he arrived at our place early in the morning and sat down in the kitchen to sharpen his knives; he brought a whole bunch of them with him: stabbing knives, cutting knives, flaying knives—every sort of knife. He spat on his whetstone and worked the edges of the blades until they were keen enough to sever a hair.

Slaughter Jonas was very talkative and friendly. He laughed loudly and doubled up when he laughed. He liked children; he liked to romp and play with us. He tickled us under the arms and pulled faces, wanting to amuse us, and he was forever trying to joke with Sigfrid and me. He said he would teach us butchering: a good trade, and not at all difficult. We could begin on sheep and calves and other small stock, for they were easiest to kill; we could manage that now if we tried. And when we had practiced on those we could start on the bigger ones: bullocks and cows.

But we looked timidly at Jonas and the long knives

155

that he was sharpening. We shunned the playful slaughterer.

Our piebald heifer fell into a rocky cleft in the copse and broke her foreleg. She couldn't get back to the cow shed on her own; her broken leg hung limply, and she couldn't walk on three. We had to haul her home on a hurdle.

"Nothing to be done for her," said Father. "Can't keep a three-legged cow. Have to send for Slaughter Jonas."

He came early in the morning, sat down in the kitchen and sharpened his knives. Father poured *brännvin* into his coffee cup several times. The slaughterer drank, and got noisy. He laughed loudly and doubled up when he laughed. As usual he joked with my brother and me, and told us we must come to him and learn the trade.

Today Sigfrid was to help Mother catch the blood. I was too little to come, but Sigfrid was big enough to make himself useful.

Father led out the piebald heifer from the cow shed. Her foreleg dangled and the hoof trailed on the ground. On three legs the heifer limped slowly forward to the place where, at the end wall of the shed, Jonas was waiting with ax and knives. Wisps of hay stuck out from her mouth; our heifer was munching the good clover hay that Mother had given her when she gave the cows their morning feed. The last gift should be of the best hay. The heifer stood, still munching, on the spot where she was to die.

Mother brought a bucket with flour at the bottom of it. Into this the blood was to flow, and be mixed with the flour. Sigfrid was to help her catch it and to stir it. He stood beside Mother, pale and awkward. He had told me he didn't want to do it. I stood some way off.

Slaughter Jonas banged the heifer on the forehead with the back of a heavy timber ax. The other foreleg, the strong one, crumpled too. Jonas struck again. The heifer gave a bellow as the forepart of her body sank down with both legs under her. Father jerked the rope that was tied round her hind hoofs to bring her over on her side. Jonas then drove a big, long knife into her throat, and a dark red jet spurted over the hand that held the knife.

I stood looking on from a distance. The heifer was still mooing faintly. I could stand no more, and ran away.

But Sigfrid had to stand by the cow-shed wall; he had to learn to catch the blood at a slaughter, Father had said. He was old enough now.

But I could not watch it. I stayed inside the house while they were slaughtering the piebald heifer, and it was a couple of hours before they finished the job. It took time to stab, flay, disembowel and carve up so big a beast as our heifer.

When I went out again Sigfrid was coming away from the slaughter, carrying the pail of blood. He was even paler now; he swallowed hard and clutched his stomach. He felt very sick.

He said, "I've thrown up. Now I've got to spew again."

Setting down the pail, he went round the corner of the cabin. When he came back he said, "Didn't you see? She tried to get up again! She heaved herself up a bit on her back legs—after they'd started skinning her. They'd done half the belly."

He looked down at the pail in his hand: "See?

That's the food we're to have. But I won't eat it. Never. And I'll never help with slaughtering again."

Next slaughtering day he stayed in bed, sick.

From the blood of our heifer Mother made a caldronful of sausages and black pudding, which were dished up for dinner. Sigfrid refused to eat any, and I wouldn't either. For I could still hear the heifer's bellow in my ears. And she had tried to get up.

Father and Mother could not think what had come over us; the pudding and sausage were so good and tasty, they melted in your mouth. They thought so, our sisters thought so, everybody in the house thought so —everybody else enjoyed the blood food. But at that meal Sigfrid and I ate only bread. Father said we ought not to have anything at all to eat until we accepted what was put before us; we must learn to appreciate our food.

And Slaughter Jonas wanted to teach us his trade. He had said that again today when he sat in the kitchen sharpening his knives. Sigfrid had whispered to me, "That old ruffian! He makes me sick."

But when as a volunteer he had done bayonet practice at the school, he wrote in the soldier's bible, "I'd have done better to stay at home and bind myself apprentice to Slaughter Jonas."

Sigfrid wanted to try different jobs, he was attracted to many trades, many kinds of life; he wanted to be in on everything on this earth. But there was one occupation that he would not take up, a kind of tool that he would not handle, a life that he could not imagine as being his own.

To that life he bound himself apprentice, and it killed him.

✤✤✤✤

I TEAR A LEAF from the calendar in my hotel room and a new one appears: September 30, 1962.

Here the hottest time of the year will soon be over. Vacationers are leaving Pine Beach and the shore is emptying of its crowds. The sea wind grows cooler, the morning mists ever denser. But the vegetation on the hills is still as scorched. The long drought continues, and the great rains won't come until December.

Yet even now an unexpected shower may cool the earth. Yesterday afternoon the Pacific displayed an outburst of rage.

I was sitting in the lobby of the Pacific when we were startled by a rainstorm from the sea; it swept in through the open French windows as if all the windows of heaven had opened too. The water crashed down, and before the porter and the bellboy working together had managed to shut the windows, a flood was pouring across the floor.

This morning the beach was covered with weed from the ocean depths, torn up by the roots and washed ashore. The sand dunes were strewn with it. Thick bands of giant kelp lay sinuous as great snakes, shiny and slippery, twelve and fifteen feet long—like deep-sea monsters hurled upon the land. Within their curves lay dead seabirds, skeletons of big fish, posts and planks torn from ships. On one red-painted piece of wood was a carved human face: perhaps an idol, a divinity in wooden form, a greeting from some tribe with a primitive religion dwelling on an opposite shore —a message from China, Australia or India? A god washed up and helpless at my feet?

After such an outburst of fury on the part of the Pacific Ocean strange things may be found upon its shores.

And when I went down for my morning dip it was still enraged. The wall of seething water advanced upon me and heaved itself with a crash against the rocks; and suddenly I was near to death.

On its way inshore a wave suddenly towered high before me, and when it rebounded from the rocks I was drawn back with it by overpowering suction. In a few seconds I was carried far out. When I saw how far, my heart beat violently: too far! "You can't make it to the shore. You're finished."

If I had kept my arms and legs still, it would have been all over within a few seconds. If for those seconds I had stopped working my arms and legs, I would have ceased to exist.

But in those moments the will to live took sole charge of my body. Reason slowed down the frantic heartbeat: "Steady, now! Only calmness can save you!" Arms and legs continued their movements, they functioned, they worked with all the strength I possessed. Hands and feet thrust against the water; the water became my support. I breathed slowly, moved my limbs with deliberation. I overtook the rollers, dived through them and came up again, was sucked back but made up lost ground. It was a slow business, very slow, but I made progress. I thrust myself forward through the sea.

My breathing failed me and I felt a hard pressure over my heart; but I saw that the distance to the beach was diminishing. A rock was coming nearer; I used it as a mark, and the sight of it gave me fresh strength. When I had only a little way to go I was near fainting; my limbs slackened, became numbed. I let my feet drop and felt for the bottom. Still none, too deep. And another great breaker came pounding in after me.

For a few seconds I lost consciousness, but when my head cleared again there was firm ground under my body. I found myself lying face down in a cleft between two rocks, and I clung on desperately with both hands. I had reached an anchorage.

I crawled up a step or two, turned onto my back and lay for a while on the beach. When I stood up my knees gave under me, and traces of dizziness remained.

I am expecting a letter from my son Albert. It didn't come this morning. Tomorrow—perhaps?

During the hour just before dusk—the great rush hour—I stand at my east window looking down Surf Street. Cars throng along it; their lines are motionless for long periods, so that from up here the street looks like one big parking lot. And some people are not yet on their way home from their day's work. I can look through the windows of Mrs. Jeffers' real-estate office and see the girls still at their typewriters. Mrs. Jeffers herself has gone to Mexico on vacation; she is staying with a woman friend in Cuernavaca. The day she left she told me about her husband: how he was held up by business in Montana and couldn't come to Pine Beach this year, but would certainly be here in the spring.

Mrs. Jeffers added that when she comes back she

wants to talk to me about something very important. What can it be? Why is she so mysterious?

Outside the entrance of the Lobster House Mr. Collins is putting up the menu for today's dinner. Every time I meet him I can see from his glazed, staring eyes that he has a stiff dose of alcohol aboard. They have a drowsy, expressionless look in them; the ray of life is missing. The proprietor of the fish restaurant has eyes like a dead, boiled fish himself. In the Småland of my childhood people would have said of him: "He looks through his whites!"

Mr. Collins hates his rival Cabrillo, whose restaurant is farther down on Surf. He told me of a wild party that was held at MEXICAN FOOD the other evening. Cabrillo has at last been granted American citizenship, and he invited his friends to his restaurant to celebrate the occasion. Everybody got drunk. One of the drunkest, a compatriot of Cabrillo's, made a speech in his honor, and in the course of it happened to disclose that the host had no right to the name that he used in Pine Beach, but had borrowed it from the Columbus of California when he moved in. Cabrillo threw him out, whereupon the party at MEXICAN FOOD, which was to celebrate Cabrillo as an American, dissolved in a free-for-all.

The Irishman of the Lobster House now wondered whether, since Cabrillo had evidently obtained his American citizenship under a false name and by false papers, the police ought not to step in and shut down his restaurant.

Maybe Mr. Collins can now rid himself of a formidable competitor.

For practical reasons Juan Rodríguez Cabrillo is concerned about his American citizenship, but he at-

162

taches more importance to his origins than any other immigrant in America that I have ever met. His pride in being Mexican is phenomenal. He is a prey to a widespread fallacy: that the mere fact of being Mexican, American, Irish or Swedish is an asset in itself. In epitaphs I read of eminent men: "He was first an American"; or "He was first a Swede." Does the fact that a person was born within a certain region of the earth guarantee him some special, positive quality?

But my new friend Mr. Jensen has never in any way stressed the fact that he is Danish. Last time I met him he said, "Today I'd like to change heads with somebody. I've got a bad headache. What a poor thing is man: only one head! And it aches. How can one escape from one's own head?"

From my window I can see the Dane's tall figure at the San Pedro intersection. This is his watch, and he is at his post. For one hour every day he puts his doctrine of love into practice and tries to rescue people from death-on-the-road: "Stop driving!" What does he do during the other twenty-three hours? I know that he was in the Korean War. He suffered a mental shock there, and when he came home he was, for several years, in a nursing home for mental patients in Los Angeles. I don't know whether the physicians consider him cured. In Pine Beach he lives with a married sister. She is said to look after him very well.

Jesus Jensen occupies my mind because he is a person who concentrates his whole life on one particular object. He is not like me, a perpetual fugitive.

Here comes what I've been waiting for: the clear tinkling of a bell calling through the traffic noise of the street. The little white truck is here.

Today it is not the ice-cream boy but a girl who

climbs down from the driver's seat. She too is dressed in white. The boy wears a pointed goblin cap; the girl is bareheaded. The bell rings, the truck stops, the ice-cream girl is here, the children come flocking. Noisily they cluster round, jostling and shoving, while the girl hands out ice-cream cones as quickly as she can. She laughs with young, fresh gaiety as the rowdy youngsters crowd up to her, tugging at her clothes. They act as if they wanted to eat her up too. But the ice-cream girl just laughs; she enjoys the mobbing, the yells, shouts and cuffing. Sun sparks gleam in her uncovered hair.

The white truck has come with joy to Surf Street.

A boy pushes forward and accidentally knocks down a little girl. The ice-cream girl grabs him by the hair and shouts something. What is she saying? "I'll . . ." She keeps hold of the boy's hair. What is she going to do?

I close my eyes and recognize them, that girl and that boy down on the street. Her hand clutches the hair at the top of his head. Into my nostrils wafts the fragrance of flowering balsam poplars around a school playground on a morning in May.

The bell rings again and the truck disappears down Surf. But the scent of balsam poplars stays with me.

I move over to the other window. The great ocean out there lies calm and pale blue, like a lake. Although yesterday the ocean rose up and menaced us with the waves of wrath, and spewed forth uprooted plants from its depths, today it lies bland and peaceful, and caresses the shore with gentle ripples born of the swell.

The sun still hangs above the horizon behind Catalina Island, and the rock fortress still rises in the west; but the first signs of dusk are here. The gleam of sunlight on the ocean starts to fade, and the water exchanges its paleness for a darker blue. The foam of the wave crests gleams against that blue, softly murmuring in a milky surge.

And this earth swings round through space, with its burden of more than three billion live human beings, including one solitary man in a hotel room. It has also carried all those who have since returned to dust. Soon the earth will turn its other side toward the sun, which during day and night divides its light between two hemispheres. Here, in the land of orange trees, the bright day is ending. But when in a few hours I seek sleep, the departing sun will be shining upon a new day in the land of the juniper.

There an old emigrant lives as if he were young.

WITH SIGFRID'S DEATH my status at home altered: I became the only son.

There were four women on our farm, but only two men: Father and I. My three sisters had to do man's work, but I never needed to do woman's work. I was now the only survivor of five sons, and so I was more important to Father and Mother than any of their daughters. My sisters felt put in the shade. Mother was anxious about me; the moment I said I had a pain anywhere she went into a panic. My sisters kept grumbling that Mother always sided with me; they called me Mother's boy, and this annoyed me. Did they have to keep flinging it at me? It made me miserable, and I tried to get even by being surly with Mother.

Emma, my eldest sister, was ten years older than I; and Linnea, my youngest, ten years younger. From babyhood Emma had had something very wrong with her ears. At night she often had earache; fluid ran out of her ears so that in the morning her pillow was stained yellow. As the years passed she became harder of hearing. It was difficult for us to talk to Emma. We had to shout to make ourselves heard, or repeat things over and over again. When she didn't hear what I said, I couldn't be bothered to repeat it. My hearing was

166

good, and I never understood what it was like for Emma. I hadn't patience enough with my deaf sister, and there was never any contact between us.

For Linnea I was the big brother. She was a fetching, funny little thing, I thought. But by the time she grew up I had left home. I never knew Linnea.

Jenny, the middle sister, was nearest to my own age; and after Sigfrid went, I turned to her. Boys were ashamed to play with girls, and only did it when no one was looking. I played with my sister Jenny even when people were looking; we stuck to each other and shared confidences. But I didn't want to get the name of "sissy"; "Mother's boy" was bad enough.

Jenny was my pretty sister. She had a clear, delicate complexion, big, wide-open eyes and lovely hair the color of ripe corn. She was shapely, with high breasts and a slender waist. She was soon sought after by the boys and took to going out with them in the evenings while still quite young. She had the merriest disposition of any of us at home.

I don't believe I ever felt any love for my parents while I was growing up, although I was in a manner attached to Mother, and this feeling strengthened with the years. There was much compassion in it. Yet she was harder than Father and had a stronger will; he could be persuaded to change his mind, but Mother never. Father was hot-tempered and hasty, but quick to repent. He was stronger than I was, and could beat me if I disobeyed him. I respected Father, but was incapable of any warmer feeling toward him. When he thrashed me I felt superior to him, since it was only by his physical strength that he could get the better of me.

I had become my parents' only son, but I still failed

to realize what this meant in my life. In the end it was to be decisive.

Since my brother's death I knew that I had become more valuable to Father and Mother, but I did not realize that they had a fixed purpose with regard to me, until one day, when they were discussing the future, Father said, "When Albert takes over the farm after us . . ."

Even then I didn't take it seriously. I didn't see that I had made a frightful discovery: namely, that my life had already been settled for me. Those who had given me life were deciding how I should live it.

Sigfrid's question on the last page of *The Infantryman's Manual* I took as being addressed to me: *Why must I die . . . ?* I had to find an answer. I had to know what had happened to him before that last day of his military service when he wrote those words.

Now I know that Father and Mother no longer withheld anything from me.

Mother said, "I think Sigfrid grieved himself into his sickness."

But no one could grieve himself into bad backache, with blood and albumen in his urine. That at least I understood.

In a little pamphlet entitled "Illness and Its Treatment," issued as a supplement to the biweekly edition of the *Evening Gazette*, I read about all kidney diseases. Sigfrid had died of one of them—but which? This I could not discover from the pamphlet. Anyhow the name of the disease was unimportant: I wanted to know how he got it.

In the little blue-and-yellow book he had left, there was a whole page of *Instructions as to Health,* by which the soldier was enjoined to be "solicitous" in the care of his body, so that he did not fall sick. Even trifling wounds and ailments, sore feet and the like, were to be "solicitously tended." The soldier was to see to it that he became neither overheated nor chilled, and that should he feel in any way ill he was to report it immediately to his superiors. The Crown and the army, Sigfrid's masters, had shown great consideration for his health; yet after only four months' service death had entered into him.

How had Sigfrid lost his healthy body while with the regiment? If anyone had taken it from him, then it was murder. I had to track down my brother's murderer.

At about this time I was reading *The Adventures of Sherlock Holmes*—the stories, published separately, cost twenty-five öre apiece—and was utterly absorbed in them; I identified myself with Holmes. I daydreamed: I would go to the regiment as a detective to discover what had happened to Sigfrid. I would assume a disguise, worm my way into the barracks of the Volunteer Training School and be a bloodhound like Holmes, who always smelled out the truth. If Sigfrid had been murdered, I would find the culprit.

Sigfrid himself had not wanted to betray anything to distress me, and so spoil our remaining time together. I now made up my mind to avenge his death.

But I was still only fourteen, and I soon realized that I was too young to visit the regiment as a detective. They would never let me in. So I decided to postpone my detective work for the time being. I could wait until I myself was called up for military service;

then I would need no disguise to enter the barracks and it would be easier to track down the truth about my brother's death.

At home one night during the autumn of 1912 I believed I had discovered some part of that truth. It was a rainy night; Father and Mother got up and put pots and pans under the holes in the old turf roof through which water dripped or poured. I had awakened too, but stayed where I was. When all the vessels were in place and the rain had stopped, my parents went back to bed.

They lay there talking to each other, thinking that I was asleep. But I lay awake and listened.

The very first words made me raise my head from the pillow. Father and Mother were talking about me:

Father: "It's a good thing that Albert's sound and healthy, now we only got him."

Mother: "If only Sigfrid hadn't enlisted."

Father: "Easy to wish that now."

Mother: "I never liked it at the time. He was too young."

Father: "He was old enough. They take 'em from eighteen."

Mother: "But he'd never been away from home. He didn't know anything about the world. And he trusted everybody."

Father: "He *wanted* to get away—you know that."

Mother: "Your cousin the corporal talked fancy about the school bein' free."

Father: "He got the same training as Nyström's own boy. Artur's a sergeant now. Our son could ha' been the same."

Mother: "But Sigfrid was sorry he joined up."

Father: "Well, he never said so. You could guess, o' course."

Mother: "What do you feel about it? Aren't *you* sorry?"

Father: "What for?"

Mother: "For what you did, what else?"

Father (in a different voice): "What did I do, then?"

Mother: "You told him he ought to. You made him enlist."

(I lifted my head higher from the pillow now; I pricked my ears, caught every word and memorized it.)

Father: "I did it for his own good, didn't I?"

Mother: "The lad was against it from the beginning. It was you and the corporal got together and persuaded him."

Father: "I just thought I was making a good future for him."

Mother: "Sigfrid was a good lad—he obeyed you and Nyström. You helped the corporal to tempt him."

Father: "I never! I never tempted him. I just wanted the best for him."

Mother: "But you helped somebody else instead, didn't you? Your cousin got the best of it. He got the recruiting pay for Sigfrid."

Father: "That's true enough. He got seventy-five kronor."

Mother: "And he got it out of our boy, the miser! He got it out of our Sigfrid."

Father: "Ay, well, I been thinking that. Nyström *is* a miser."

Mother: "Now I feel as if Sigfrid was sold. Just, exactly that, *sold*."

When Mother said that, I put my hands over my ears, wriggled as far down in bed as I could and pulled the bedclothes over my head. I don't know what else Father and Mother said to each other; I stopped up my ears, I didn't want to hear any more; I couldn't. . . .

Sold—*sold*—SOLD.

I had heard enough.

🌲

When I ask myself why I emigrated, I go back to that rainy night fifty years ago, when my parents talked about Sigfrid. Every word of theirs that I caught I stowed carefully away in my memory.

My brother obeyed Father and Uncle Nyström when he enlisted. He was sold to the regiment. Uncle Nyström was paid for his healthy young body: seventy-five kronor. Sigfrid never got that body back, but Uncle Nyström kept the money.

Sigfrid had been an obedient son, and for that reason he lived only nineteen years. But the same thing was not going to happen to me. No one would do to me what had been done to Sigfrid. Something inside me rose up and rebelled against it: No! No ! No! I would not let them do it. You are here on earth just this one time! Take good care of your life! Look after it! Don't let anyone take it from you!

I was not going to obey anybody, neither Father nor Mother nor anyone else—neither parents nor any other relatives. I would take care of myself, not allow myself to be persuaded or guided by anyone. I would pay no attention to the fourth commandment—or any other commandment; I wouldn't listen to anybody. Nobody was going to profit by me. I would be ruled by myself alone.

Of late I had become my parents' only son; now I became also their disobedient one. I defied them. Almost every day I opposed them in something. Finally I opposed so far as to emigrate to America. I left them; I left home, village and native land. I abandoned the juniper country for the country of orange trees— because I wanted to live long on the earth.

✝✝✝✝

My awakening this morning in my room at the Pacific differed from other awakenings: I seemed to have heard a knocking at the door. Still half asleep, I shouted, "Come in!" I shouted twice.

But the door of Room 20 did not open. Nobody came in, and in the corridor outside there was absolute silence. I sat up in bed and realized that the knocking was coming from within the room: One of my chairs bumped the floor with its forefeet, and the little chest of drawers near the head of my bed was rocking to and fro and hitting the wall. My furniture was on the move.

I shot out of bed, knowing exactly what had happened or was happening; I had experienced it before. At some time or other every year we get a reminder that we live within a seismic zone of the earth.

The furniture was still again. But the shocks usually come in series, at varying intervals. So long as the chairs in my room remained on their legs, nothing had happened. But the next tremor might be ten or twenty times as violent.

When inanimate things in a room begin moving and wake a person up, that person should at once get out. And I did the first thing one does do when wakened by an earthquake: I dressed quickly and ran downstairs to the hall. The elevator would have been slower.

The hall clock pointed to five minutes to eight. At the reception desk a surprising calm prevailed. The porter was on the telephone, and I heard that he was speaking to a glazier. One of the French windows had smashed and the wind was blowing in. Broken glass crunched under my feet as I hurried over. The porter took the receiver from his ear and cried out to me in warning, "Take it easy, Mr. Carlson!"

An elderly woman came rushing after me down the stairs, screaming loudly. She hadn't waited to fasten her dressing gown over her bosom. Her bedside table with the breakfast tray on it had overturned and rolled across the floor of her room. Men and women may get hysterical for less. But the porter maintained a professional calm. The agitated lady was promised a fresh breakfast if she would kindly return to her room. There was nothing whatever to worry about. Just a little earth tremor. Absolutely nothing to be afraid of.

The hysterical guest calmed down. The bellboy opened the elevator door for her and she went up again to her room. In the breakfast room off the hall a solitary man was drinking coffee, entirely absorbed in his newspaper. On the floor lay a few broken tumblers from which another morning drink—orange juice—flowed golden-yellow across the floor. In the hall a maid began sweeping up the glass fragments from the broken window. The porter said that the glazier was coming right away.

I went outside. When the earth starts to become restless, one should get out under the open sky, and that morning I wanted no other roof above me. The Pacific Hotel is several stories high; but the deserted, empty heavens where God no longer dwells cannot fall down and bury me.

I went north along Surf Street. Stores and offices had not yet opened, and motor traffic was sparse. A big truck from the street-cleaning department drove past, watering the street from long, thick hoses, and flooding the gutters. The street was its usual self; this was a morning like any other morning in Pine Beach. I saw no anxious faces. The shock had lasted only a few moments and perhaps had gone unnoticed by most of the inhabitants, so that they had no fear that it might be the first of a series.

I continued along Ocean Avenue and Victor Hugo Street. On Victor Hugo I always imagine that I may encounter Jean Valjean, of *Les Misérables*. In a building of the old Spanish style I saw a couple of men busy with some broken windows. A minor earth tremor makes work chiefly for the glaziers.

Where Victor Hugo ends, the highway takes over, running here through a wood of eucalyptus trees with barkless trunks. The town is a close neighbor of the primeval forest. I walk a little way into the morning-cool shade of those mighty trees before turning back.

When I get back to Surf Street, Mrs. Boles has just opened her drugstore. I go in and she hands me the Los Angeles *Times*.

"What's going to happen now, Mr. Carlson?"

Her voice is unsteady; she is much afraid today.

I glance round the drugstore, but see no trace of the earth tremor—not so much as a cracked windowpane.

"But nothing here has been damaged, has it, Mrs. Boles?"

She stares at me blankly. "I'm talking about Cuba. Don't you know? Look! Read this!"

And she points to the gigantic black headlines con-

176

fronting me on the front page of my paper: NEW WORLD CRISIS. RUSSIAN ROCKET BASES IN CUBA. NUCLEAR THREAT! Last October the Russians exploded their doomsday bombs. What bombs will go off this year? What will happen this October?

"Do you think this is the end, Mr. Carlson?"

I answer, "This morning when I woke up, I thought it was the end."

I buy a couple of other morning papers and return to the Pacific. The porter hands me my mail, but *the* letter is not among it. I wrote to him in July and it is now October, and he has not answered.

Every morning there is a letter that doesn't come. There is one person in the world whom I want to come closer to, and I cannot reach him.

The ground beneath my home in the universe stirred slightly within a small area; it trembled for a few seconds. It was no earthquake, just a little tremor. A chair rocked, a table fell over, windows were broken. That was all.

Yet it may be a preliminary warning. A crack in the crust of the earth widens, the ground splits and opens. One may wake one night lying under the rubble of a house, wake in pain, pinned between beams, unable to get out or even move; wake deep down in a dark hole with one's body broken. No ray of daylight reaches one, nor the least sound of other people. One shouts for help, but reaches no one with one's voice. One lies there day after night after day, alone with one's pain, unable to soothe it or put an end to it.

The chest of drawers by my bed knocked against the

177

wall this morning, and woke me. I shall find it hard to sleep tonight.

I am not afraid of death but of what may happen to me before it comes. *Afterward* doesn't frighten me; *before* does.

It is to the fear of this *before* that I trace the experience I had the other night. It was not a dream; I was aware, I felt, I lived it all intensely. It was reality.

I was lying in bed and it was night-dark in the room. All at once it was bright day and the sun shone into my eyes. In the sunshine I saw a man standing up on a high mound under a clear, arching sky. He stood motionless with his back to me, and his limbs were bound; broad, strong leather straps had been wound tightly round his arms and legs so that he could move neither hand nor foot. On each side of him stood a policeman holding his elbows. He was wedged as in a vise between the two cops, who carried revolvers in their leather holsters.

Before them on the mound a cross had been erected, and on the cross hung my Scandinavian compatriot, Jesus Jensen. His head and feet were bare, he was dressed in his long coat, and his arms were outstretched along the crossbeam. His thick, bushy hair had the outline of a spiky crown of thorns against the sky beyond.

The Dane was hanging on the cross, but he was not crucified. No nails had been driven through his body. The palms of his hands were outspread on the crossbeam, but there were no nails in them or in his bare feet at the lower end of the cross.

How could Jesus Jensen stay up there? How was he fastened?

He looked down and laughed aloud; his laughter

rang out over the hillock, and he shouted to the men below: "Look! It doesn't hurt! Why should it? I'm not nailed. They can't drive any nails into me—no nail would go in. For I'm the Son of God! Nobody understands that, but I am. And they can't knock nails into the Son of God. So I feel nothing. Why should I?"

Jesus Jensen on the cross jeered at those who stood below it: "No one can take my life from me."

Two men in overalls, who looked like the laborers one sees near the sign saying MEN AT WORK, were digging a hole beside the cross, and throwing up a little heap of earth with their spades. When the hole was finished, they took up a tall post and a short crosspiece.

The men were putting up another cross.

The bound man between the two powerful policemen had been dumb. Now he opened his mouth and cried, "That other one! Who is he?"

The policemen made no reply; it was as if they had not heard him. The revolver holsters dangled against their sturdy thighs and their hands caressed the weapons voluptuously.

The man cried louder, "That other one there! Who is he? Who?" But no one answered him.

The two men in overalls went on with their work. They prepared the hole; they nailed the crossbeam to the post, lifted the cross and set it upright in the hole.

Two crosses now stood side by side on the mound, one of them empty.

The man between the constables shouted more loudly and repeated his question: "Who?"

Then he was answered. Jesus Jensen spoke to him from the cross: "You're not the Son of God! You're just a man, so it's going to . . . Listen to me: It's going to . . ."

He gave a roar of mocking laughter that shook the post.

The cops took a firmer hold on their prisoner's elbows and began to drag him forward. He resisted; I saw him twisting his body between the two big men, tearing at the straps and trying to free his hands, bracing his feet against the ground. He was struggling with all his might. But he was helpless against his guards. They dragged him up the slope.

There was not far to go. At the top two men stood waiting with other tools in their hands.

Suddenly the mound with its two crosses sank down below the ground, and all that remained was darkness. Everything I'd seen had vanished: Jesus Jensen, the policemen, the workmen in overalls—and the prisoner.

I never saw the bound man's face; his back had been toward me all the time. Yet all the time I knew who he was.

In my hotel room I sank back and lay safe in bed again. No danger threatened me, no one near me wanted to do me any harm. But I had not dreamed, I had not returned from the unreal; I had come from one reality to another. This thing had happened in some chamber of my brain. For it is there that it lives, my dread of *before*: before I return whence I came, before I become inaccessible once more, before all is over and transformed and has become what yesterday is today. Today is soon tomorrow, tomorrow is soon today and yesterday; tomorrow is soon fifty years gone by.

Of the time that passed before I existed one may perhaps say that it was as long as that which will come after. I was then in that same inaccessible chamber that awaits me again. I have no ugly memories of my sojourn in that place. Where nothing is, nothing can be evil.

For the time being I am still on the quaking little strip of uncertainty, and to dispel my dread of the *before* that is to come, which darkens the present, I summon up the past.

IN A LARGE ENVELOPE marked "Family Papers" I keep a bundle of documents which I took charge of at my father's death: contracts, auction catalogues, wills. Information about people who lived before my day is recorded here, and things that they have left tell of them and their daily life. Here are no fables or legends, only facts; by means of these things I may *know*.

In the same envelope is the inventory of Sigfrid's possessions. As he was over eighteen at the time of his death, the law required that his effects should be listed and distributed among his heirs. Living people are very particular when dealing with dead people's property.

The document was examined and approved by the district court and adorned with large stamps:

INVENTORY

in respect of the late home son *Axel Sigfrid Karls-son,* of 1/16 mantal in the village of Källenbäck in the parish of Sjöhult, said inventory having this day been by order completed by the undersigned;

Suit of clothes	15 kronor	
1 Pair Top Boots	10 "	
Ditto Ankle Boots	6 "	
1 Trunk	12 "	
Sundry Books	25 "	
1 Purse	1 "	
Cash residue	2 "	55 öre.
Total:	71 kronor	55 öre.

The suit that the village tailor made for Sigfrid before he went away was too big for me, but Father tried it on one Sunday morning before going to church, and it fitted him almost perfectly, except that the trousers were rather too long. Father used these clothes until they were worn out, but the boots were put aside for me until my feet should be big enough for them. Afterward I wore them for years until they too wore out. My eldest sister Emma was given the trunk when she left home. "Sundry Books" I took over with joy; no one else in my parents' home cared about them. But they had been valued at far too low a figure: 25 kronor for the lot. Sigfrid used to send off for big parcels of secondhand 25-öre books which he got for 10, but he had also bought many volumes at one krona and even more. He had sacrificed hundreds of kronor for the "Sundry Books" that were now estimated at 25.

Something of the living Sigfrid stayed in our home in the dead things he left behind. He was in the suit that Father wore, the shoes that I wore, the books I read. I wondered whether he had wanted to remain among us in that way.

Missing from the inventory was Sigfrid's watch that Father had given me. If the letter of the law had been observed, Father would have been prosecuted for misappropriation of his son's effects.

Another item, and one that perhaps would have had a higher value set upon it than any of his other belongings, was also missing from the stamped paper: his gun. The sporting gun that Father gave him is not included. "1 Gun, old Muzzle-loader . . . — kronor."

These omissions tell me more about Sigfrid than everything that is set down; and in my wanderings with him through memory they bring me to a certain woodcock evening in the spring of 1910.

In his youth Father loved hunting. He shot hares and birds. But when our hunting dog died after eating fox poison, Father never got another gundog, and the kennel remained empty. That put an end to the shooting of hares, which cannot be hunted without a dog. He still went after capercailzie and blackcock, but what he liked best was the woodcock season in the spring. He never missed a single year. When one stood on the lookout in the evening twilight, the swift-winged woodcock appeared for no more than a second or two, so that in this sport the contest was more equal than in hunting the hare.

Father's gun, a fine muzzle-loader, had belonged to his father, and he now gave it to Sigfrid for his seventeenth birthday. The old family gun should pass to the eldest son, who was now old enough to handle one, and Father would show him how to use it. They would go out together on the first evening of the woodcock season.

Sigfrid had never shown any enthusiasm for hunting or shooting and showed none now in spite of having a gun of his own. Before, he had had a crossbow, which was no good for shooting animals, but it had been enough for him. I was keener on woodcock shooting than my brother, and begged and pleaded with my father to be allowed to come too. Little boys were only in the way at a shoot, he said, but I might come if I held my tongue and kept quiet on watch.

So we went, father and sons, down to our copse, and there we took up our stand in a long glade where bushes grew. This was the best place for woodcock, Father said. This evening he would shoot and Sigfrid would learn to load. It took practice to load a gun through the muzzle; it meant handling ramrod, powder horn, shot bag, caps and wads. Father carried the caps in a matchbox and old newspapers in his pockets for wads. He showed Sigfrid—he poured powder and shot into the muzzle, rammed down the wads with the ramrod and placed the cap under the hammer: "Remember it's lightly cocked!" Then he fired into the air and Sigfrid had to reload.

My brother spilled powder on the ground when he was pouring it from the horn; he fumbled with the wads and was clumsy. He was not quick enough, Father said; a marksman needed nimble fingers. Plenty of woodcock could have flown by while he was loading.

It was still a bit early, he said. Too light. But one had to take up one's position in good time.

We stood under a young spruce, Father with his forefinger on the trigger and his thumb on the lightly cocked hammer, and Sigfrid and I on each side of him. We were ready.

"Help me to listen, boys," said Father.

He had become a little hard of hearing, and so was no longer a good shot with woodcock, he told us.

We stood perfectly still. Three faces were turned upward, tensely listening, awaiting the bird of twilight.

"If you hear a noise like *knorr-knips-knarr,* tell me!"

The sportsman cocks his gun when he hears the knorring and knipsing of the woodcock; the cry of the twilight bird costs it its life.

It was still a little too light, Father thought. The sun had dipped behind the tops of the spruce firs, but its radiance lingered on the earth, and over our heads was the bright expanse of the May evening. Tonight earth and sky had drawn near each other. On the firs of the clearing the young cones showed bright as flowers. Delicate birches stood in bud and would soon open their leaves. The ground was speckled with anemones that opened their petals under the bushes. A light shower had just fallen, and there came a sparkling and glittering from leaves and fir needles. The rain had washed over ground and growth and released their fragrance: There was a smell of resin, of running sap from the trunk of the spruce, sap seething in the bark, and of opening birch buds.

We stood beneath a young spruce in the midst of colors, scents and light. It was very quiet in our glade. We were silent; we were not to talk but to listen. A single sound came from the ground about us: Among the thickets the water had run together into a brook that rippled and splashed.

But the atmosphere was filled with sound and life. It was May; it was a woodcock evening and the evening of many other birds. When the sun disappeared, their songs broke out from the woods. The song thrush fluted; at the top of a fir sat a cuckoo calling and every now and again clucking as if something had got stuck in its throat. It was a "west cuckoo, the best cuckoo," but this was not the first we had heard this year, so we paid no attention to the direction it came from; it meant nothing. In the distance a bird whose name I did not know uttered a laughing cry; it laughed continuously, and I wondered at what.

A blackcock gave its unceasing call—the bird with a rippling brook in its throat; he was in a distant tree-top. But from the thicket close by came a muffled, hissing noise. I whispered to Sigfrid, "Is there a snake in there?" But he said it was only a blackbird.

A shot rang out from a neighboring enclosure: the flight had begun. Tension rose: this was hunting. The fresh smell of resin entered my nostrils. Last year's brown, drooping bracken clung to my wooden shoes. I waited, listened, peered and watched.

With all my senses keyed up I experienced that woodcock evening, an evening of delight. I was among all that lived, and I myself was one of those lives. I forgot our purpose there.

I was supposed to be helping Father to listen, but there were so many birds in the woods that the noises in the air confused me and I could not distinguish the *knorr-knips* of the woodcock from all the other bird voices.

"If only they'd keep quiet a bit," said Father. "They make so much noise I can't hear."

More shots rang out. On this first evening of the woodcock season many other people were on the watch, thumb on hammer, listening and waiting like us.

"I heard a *knorr*," Sigfrid whispered to Father.

I heard nothing, nor did Father. He cocked the gun, swung round and looked up in the air in all directions, but did not shoot.

"I spotted her behind the treetops. Too far."

At that moment something happened. There was a rustling at the edge of the glade and a four-footed animal crept slowly forth out of the bushes. It was furry, about the size of a piglet, and it looked rather like one. Its head was striped black and white, its back was speckled with gray and ended with a short rump. A little pig with a furry coat. It halted a few paces from us, lifted its snout and sniffed the air. A bit of brown bracken had clung to its shaggy back.

Father saw the beast, but kept his gun still. I whispered, "Shoot!" But just then I made a slight movement, and with a couple of long hops it was back in the thicket.

"A badger," murmured Father. "I can't shoot badgers with woodcock shot."

Before he had finished speaking, the first twilight bird flew over us. *Knorr-knips—knorr-knips*—the sound filled the air. I caught sight of a long beak and a pair of whirlwind wings showing like a black cross against the light sky. But like an arrow it vanished behind the treetops.

Father's jaw dropped. He had not even cocked his gun. "I wasn't looking. That damned badger put me off."

From close at hand two shots cracked out in quick succession: someone with a double-barreled gun, Father explained. If he missed with one he might hit with the other.

Then the woodcock's call was over us again. Father swung his gun barrel up, hardly giving himself time to put the butt to his shoulder and aim.

The shot broke the silence. The woodcock halted suddenly in its flight, its wings moving as before. Then it turned in another direction and flew on. In a moment or two the twilight bird was out of sight behind two tall firs.

"Missed! I aimed badly."

"He flew faster after the shot," said Sigfrid. He didn't sound disappointed at Father's failure.

The shot came back from the woods in a ringing echo. Afterward all was quiet; the woods held their breath. I inhaled the smell of gunsmoke. Father took powder horn, shot bag and the box of caps, and Sigfrid made wads which Father rammed down the barrel. Loading had to be done quickly. Father was full of the fire of the chase, and I felt the joy of it too and its excitement.

But my elder brother seemed unmoved; he was not absorbed in it as I was.

"No luck this evening," said Father. "It was that badger. If it hadn't been for that, I'd've got one."

The sound of shots was coming now from all directions, often two in quick succession; the new double-barreled shotguns had become popular in the district.

Darkness fell slowly over our glade. The tops of the spruce firs blackened against the sky; birdsong began to die away and quietness descended on the woods. In the west blood-red streaks shot across the sky. The birch saplings shone yellow-white in the dusk. We were swathed in deepening twilight and could be seen only from close at hand. We stood hidden under the spruce like poachers. But we had a right to be there on our own land in our own copse, and the bird we were after was lawful game today.

Cracks from other guns were coming now at longer intervals, and for a while nothing happened in our glade. The best flights were over, Father said. Sigfrid in a whisper asked if it wasn't time to go home.

But Father didn't want to go home empty-handed; it would be a disgrace to return from the first woodcock evening without so much as a feather.

Then the cry came again, and the bird appeared be-

189

tween two treetops. This time Father was prepared. With his gun barrel he followed the bird in its flight and took careful aim before firing.

The bird's flight ended at the instant the shot crashed out; its wings curved and folded, its beak turned downward, and with a slanting movement the woodcock fell into the thicket beside us.

"Got her!" murmured Father delightedly. "Go and find her."

He began reloading while Sigfrid and I rushed into the bushes. I had seen that it had fallen by a young birch, and crouching under the brushwood and branches, we hunted around the tree. It was dark in there; we crept between the bushes, pushed aside branches, felt with our hands over the moss and roots. The woodcock is a little bird, gray-brown like the ground. We groped about, but grasped only dry leaves, and sharp twigs pricked our fingers. Our hands found no bird.

Father came after us. "She fell down here, by the birch."

All three of us searched, Sigfrid the most eagerly, but in the bushes round the birch it was as dark as a cellar. We ought to have had a light. We broke twigs, tore up the moss; we crept about on our knees groping. But three seekers found no more than two had done.

"We ought to've had a dog," said Father. "He'd've found her."

We missed Jäger that evening.

But Sigfrid and I searched about like a couple of keen-scented hounds. With our hands we searched every inch of the ground within a radius of many yards. At one moment we heard a rustle some way off, as if something were moving among the dry leaves. We dashed toward the sound, but we heard it no more and sought in vain. Not so much as a feather did we find, far less a whole bird.

We went on searching for some time until Father said, "No good. Let's go home."

"We must find her first," said Sigfrid.

Father explained that the bird had been winged, but that if she could use her legs she might have run anywhere once she reached the ground. She must have run off and hidden somewhere, but it was no good looking for her any longer that night: too dark, thought Father.

Sigfrid said, "If she's winged, we've got to find her."

"It's too late."

It was quite dark now, and there was nothing more we could do. The shoot was over.

We set off home. A straggler flew across the road and Father shot at it but missed.

For the rest of the way he was sulky and silent: a rotten evening, no luck, not a feather—what a start to the season!

⚜

When we got up and dressed next morning Sigfrid was bleary-eyed and yawned sleepily.

"I slept badly last night. Kept thinking of that woodcock down in the copse."

He had dreamed about the wounded twilight bird that we had failed to find: He had seen it crouching under a stone in a deep hole—a little body with heavy lead shot in it and broken wings, a flightless bird. How must a bird feel when it couldn't fly, couldn't use its wings? Like a paralyzed person who couldn't use his

191

legs? A little forsaken life had lain all night in its hiding place in the woods with no company but the lead in its body—lead from the gun that was now to be Sigfrid's.

The woodcock was lying there in its agony waiting for some creature to sniff its way to the hiding place—waiting for the jaws of a beast of prey.

A shot from Sigfrid's gun had hurled the bird out of its flight and hurt it, and he felt partly to blame. Now he was going to look for the poor little thing so that it need suffer no longer. Would I go with him and help him, now that it was daylight?

Sigfrid and I went down to the copse and resumed our search in the dense thicket where the bird had disappeared. The daylight didn't help: We couldn't find the slightest trace of the wounded bird.

"The badger must have eaten her up," I thought.

"Or a fox," said Sigfrid, "or perhaps—" He broke off, was silent for a little and then added, "Or perhaps she's still lying there in the hole—and—yes, for how long?"

We went home with our errand unfulfilled. Sigfrid said, "No. I'm not ever going to shoot anything."

He never loaded the gun that Father had given him, and never went shooting. During the summer that he was ill Father asked him several times about the gun; the old muzzle-loader was no longer in the house, and he could not find it. I don't know what Sigfrid told him.

But a couple of years after Sigfrid's death I was looking for something in the corner of the woodshed, where we used to throw bits and pieces of junk that were of no further use; and here in a big heap of scrap iron, hidden among worn or broken tools, I found his gun. The old weapon was verdigrised and rusted—unusable. It belonged here among all the other worn out things that had accumulated on the scrap heap in the woodshed.

And I possess a stamped paper certifying that Sigfrid left no implements of death behind him.

✝✝✝✝

THE YEARS BETWEEN MY CONFIRMATION and emigration I felt were being wasted. Thousands of days trickled away and nothing was changed for me: I remained a home son. Later—much later—I was to regard those years as having been put to better use than any others of my life. It may be that I have never known what I had while I had it—never known what I possessed until I lost it. My time is not happy until it is over. Those years that I squandered through discontent should have seemed the most joyous of my life, and what I threw away ought to have been preserved.

My existence at home differed little from that of other farmers' sons brought up in a remote place. Every weekday hard physical work, every night deep and healthy sleep. In my free time I took full part in all the fun of youth; I danced through hundreds of nights—danced many, many miles. In time I overcame my shyness of girls and had my first sexual experiences, which only made me yearn for more—and more satisfying ones. Katrin married and left the dance while she was still young. She had a number of children and was a matronly farmer's wife. I felt nothing for her as the married woman, but my disembodied love for the schoolgirl remained with me.

A couple of thousand days passed without sorrow—

or what now seems to me sorrow. But I was a home son, dependent on my parents—I who was to be a scholar, learned in history; I who had determined to find out all that had happened on the earth before my own time! Year after year went by and I learned so little—I who was to write history textbooks. For Father and Mother opposed me, and how was I to achieve learning on my own?

Sigfrid's fate was a warning. I steered clear of free schooling. I tried to acquire knowledge by myself. I read everything I could lay my hands on. I took correspondence courses, and in the summer I studied with a university student from the village when he came home on vacation. But my studies were sporadic and unmethodical; they were mere childish attempts to break away. I got nowhere. Before I could be admitted through the Portals of Learning I would have to take the university entrance exam, and that could not be done in the kitchen at home.

Father and Mother asked what was the point of all this studying, as I would eventually inherit their land and be a farmer? For that is what they had decided. They had set that as my goal and it could not be altered.

Both Father and Mother had grown up in great poverty and battled with it for many years. When they bought the farm they were in debt for more than half the purchase price, and had to pay a hundred kronor in interest on it twice a year. That mortgage felt like a rope round his neck, Father used to say; twice a year the noose was drawn tight. The days immediately before payment date were always anxious ones in my parents' home, and usually five or ten of the hundred kronor were lacking.

But from 1914 onward poor smallholders in neutral Sweden were helped by the First World War. All the produce they could sell rose in price; all that was fit to eat became so valuable that in the end there was none to be bought. Money came into our home. Father sold woodland to pay off the last of the debt on our little place, and we were released from the mortgage.

After many years of dogged saving, striving, toil and labor my parents were out of debt and owners of their land. And this land that they slaved for, sweated for, sacrificed themselves for, could not be allowed to pass from the family. It must be tilled and tended by one of the children. If it passed into the hands of strangers, all their struggles would have been to no avail; their life of toil would have had no purpose; they would have lived it in vain.

Therefore Father and Mother required me to stay at home. They would hear of nothing else. A clear and explicit command.

I thought that one of my three sisters might marry and take over the farm, for it could make no difference whether Father was succeeded by a son or a son-in-law. By this time it seemed unlikely that there would be any son-in-law through Emma, the eldest. She was very deaf, which was a grave defect. No man would want a wife whom he had to yell at to make himself heard. Farmers wanted unblemished wives. But my sister Jenny was pretty and gay and popular with boys. I told her to marry a fellow who would take over the farm; then I wouldn't have to stay at home. "Promise me," I said. "Get Father and Mother a son-in-law, and then I can go."

Jenny laughed at me, but promised. She would do

what I wanted, she promised faithfully. Nothing easier; she had plenty to choose from. She laughed merrily: What sort did I think she should have? Fair or dark, blue-eyed or brown-eyed, fat or thin?

But my pretty sister broke her promise to me. She was in her twentieth year when her course of life was determined. She changed, she lost her gaiety, she became silent and red-eyed.

It was Mother who told me about it: Jenny was going to have a child—and in just a couple of months. There would be no marriage: Jenny had no one to marry.

Mother didn't say much to me about what had happened to my sister, but I realized that she and Father had pronounced stern judgment on her. They had always warned Jenny against running around with boys at night, telling her that no good would come of it; but she had paid no attention, and now the "no good" was here.

The rest of us at home were all to be ashamed of what had happened to Jenny: She was going to have a bastard. And this was something that concerned everyone in Källebäck, for everybody seemed to be talking about it. All condemned her—mothers of girls who were not pregnant with illegitimate children, and girls who had envied my pretty sister her way with boys.

Outwardly Father and Mother pretended unconcern. Mother said, "Our Jenny's not the best, nor yet the worst. She's not the first, nor she won't be the last."

I refused to be ashamed of my sister. I beat up a boy who remarked he was sorry he hadn't been the one to get her with child. What Jenny had done did not seem wrong to me; she only let a boy come too close to her,

197

into her, although she wasn't married to him. I had been close to girls in that same way, and one girl had even surrendered her virginity to me. I was the last person to condemn my sister. I would have liked to tell her so, but we couldn't talk to each other about this; we were both too shy. It was something that could not be mentioned between brother and sister.

The young man who had got her with child was assistant to the surveyor who had recently been measuring the roads through Sjöhult parish. This work was over now; the boy had left the district and sent no word. Jenny expected a letter for a long time. But I never heard her say an ill word about the man who had let her down. She said, "I liked Sven and I trusted him. We were to have been married in the spring."

And when spring came, Jenny had a baby girl. After that she lived only for her child; and in time Father and Mother also grew fond of Jenny's little girl and were deeply attached to her. They made more fuss over their granddaughter than they had over their own children.

So in the end joy came from the baby instead of sorrow. Its birth was the happiest event at home between my confirmation and emigration.

But my sister Jenny could not keep her promise to me and bring a son-in-law into the farm, for now she could never get married. There she was with a child; she was disgraced.

Mother said it was the prettiest girls who were the first to be disgraced.

And it was true that my sister Jenny would not be the last.

So now there were five women at home, and still only two men. Father said we ought to have been better

198

matched; now there was too much of one kind and not enough of the other.

And half of the menfolk was wishing himself away.

In 1917, the last year but one of the war, I joined the coast artillery at Karlskrona, where as an unwilling and rebellious recruit I did my military service. I did not join the regiment where Sigfrid fell ill and where I had once intended to investigate how this had happened—an idea that now seemed to me childish. I felt I would never learn the whole truth about my brother, and was becoming resigned to this.

Our relative, the corporal first class, never came to see us now. Uncle Nyström had not been in our house since that Sunday morning when he brought Sigfrid the recruiting form. I understood: My parents did not want to see him in the house. I had not heard his name mentioned at home since the night of the rain.

But Sergeant Nyström came on leave several times a year. "My Artur," the corporal's son, arrived at Easter, in midsummer and at Christmas, and appeared in front of the church in his fine uniform. He was handsomely built and looked well even in plain clothes. Even before he joined up he was known as the Girls' Delight: a name given him by envious boys. When he visited his home district as an N.C.O. of good standing, there was much talk about him, and he was the king of every dance. Girls neglected their fiancés for him. But he was said to have a rich fiancée in town; no farmer's daughter was good enough, naturally, for Sergeant Nyström.

I did not want to meet Artur any more. We saw each other often while Sigfrid was alive, but now I avoided him. I stayed away from the dances or parties that I knew he was to attend. For he wore a uniform that I could not bear to see. Artur wore the clothes of Sigfrid's regiment, of my brother's service, with the same regimental number—I.21—on the shoulder straps, and I felt as if he were walking about and swaggering over my dead brother.

Before my mind's eye I could always see Uncle Nyström at our table, dipping his mustache into the coffee cup with the *brännvin* in it: "Look at my Artur!" The proud father. "See how a boy can get on when he joins up! He's in command, an N.C.O.; he's in charge of the recruits. The richest farmer's son must obey him. Look at my son!"

But there was one boy who did not come home in a smart sergeant's uniform; he returned in a common civilian suit made by our shaky-handed old village tailor. He came home as he had left, in the same old clothes, with his belongings in the same little wooden trunk. But one thing he had acquired while he was away: a paper from the M.O. Look here, Father and Mother. Look at your son!

I did not want to meet Artur.

And who had been given seventy-five kronor for measuring and enrolling a recruit? "Fine!" he had said. "No one to touch you, boy." "Sigfrid has never been ill," Father had said.

Accepted. Here's payment in cash for the corporal.

"Your money or your life!" cried the highwaymen in the stories. Not hard to choose: money was much more valuable than life; and I was now old enough to grasp this.

So I would never have anything to do with money, or concern myself with it in whatever work I did. I no longer knew what I was going to be, or what line of work I was best suited for, but there was one thing I could never imagine myself being, and that was a businessman. Anything in the world but that. For it might happen that in dealing with affairs one was dealing in human lives.

Ever since I was small, Father and Mother had impressed upon me: Be careful with money. Never buy anything you don't need—only things you really must have. Take good care of every penny.

The point was that only a person with money could be free of it, and not have to think and worry about it. That I had found out, as a home son. So I would earn enough money to be free of it; and that I could do in another country, as many others had. In Sjöhult parish there were plenty of Swedish-Americans who had gone to the States in their youth and returned financially independent. And I was of age now, so my parents could not prevent me from taking out emigration papers. Many years had been wasted on the home son, and it was high time I got rid of him.

I would go to America and come back a free man, able to do what I liked. I would run away from the home son.

The most painful memory of my youth is of an evening in April, 1920, when my ticket to America came.

Unknown to my parents, I had written to one of Mother's brothers in Iron Mountain, Michigan. He was both well-off and generous; every Christmas he sent Mother twenty-five dollars, and one Christmas he sent ten dollars to me. Now I asked him for a ticket to his new country, where I wanted to try my luck too.

It was one of the last days in April, in the middle of the spring work. We planted our potatoes in the field next to the house; it was a cold, late spring, and I remember snow falling in the furrows. Father drove the wooden plough: April snow is as good as sheep manure, he said when it began to fall. But my hands were cold and my fingers numb as I followed him along the furrow and put in the potatoes.

As soon as we had stopped work in the field for that day, I hurried to get the mail, not even waiting to wash my muddy hands. I was expecting something important from America, and had inquired about it several days before. This evening it had come, and the envelope contained what I was waiting for. My uncle had not let me down.

As I fingered the ticket, I saw that I ought to have washed my hands after the potato planting; there was now a muddy stain on the paper and it wouldn't come off. The imprint of the earth from my father's potato field remained on my ticket to America.

I sat at supper with the others in the kitchen with the ticket in my jacket pocket. The time had come to break the news to my father and mother, for I had to start getting ready at once. I was to sail from Göteborg in a fortnight.

I told them quite quietly, almost casually; I told Father and Mother what I had in my pocket.

They heard that their last remaining son was to emigrate to America.

Mother resigned herself; it was the only time I ever knew her to change her mind. I was gladdened and surprised by the way she took it. She heaved a deep sigh and said, "Well, there it is, I s'pose. Nothing to be done about it. May God be with you, Albert."

But Father scared me.

He was just ladling out porridge from the dish onto his plate, but the hand with the spoon in it stopped halfway. Porridge slopped out of it onto the table. Father sat motionless as a block of wood, glaring at me. His great coarse hand clutched the spoon convulsively, as if it were a support that he had to cling to. He just glowered at me, sitting perfectly still for a minute or so.

Then his mouth began to move; but he couldn't speak—he stammered, and uttered only syllables and broken words.

Suddenly he stood up, and so violently that he nearly overturned the table. He regained his speech and pronounced whole words.

"What the . . . what the devil are you saying, boy? God damn it. . . . No! Hell, no!"

Mother cried out, "Don't—don't talk like that."

"To America . . . says he's going to America . . . my only . . . no, I won't have it, by God, I won't."

Then I answered my father in those terrible words that I have regretted all down the years: "You can't forbid me. I won't obey. Sigfrid's life was wrecked through obeying you, and that's not going to happen to me." No sooner were the words out of my mouth than I would have recalled them if I could.

Father's mouth still moved, but he said nothing more. He looked at me and he looked round the kitchen, searching; he looked at the wall where the stove rake and bread peel hung, at the long iron poker and at the pile of big logs in the chimney corner.

He was looking for a weapon.

I had not been thrashed by my father since confirmation. But now he was looking round for a weapon, and going over to the woodpile he picked out one of the thickest logs.

Mother sprang up, and pulled and tugged at my arm. "Get out! For God's sake! Run!"

I was grown up, I was a man, I would do as I pleased; I would not run away because of Father. I sat where I was.

I waited. Mother was distracted with terror. But I sat where I was.

There was a crash that shook the kitchen.

Father had tossed the big log to the floor so violently that it sounded like a shot. Then I jumped up too. But Father took a couple of long strides to the door—he himself was running out of the kitchen. Our kitchen was fairly large, the largest room in the house, but it was too small for the two men at that moment; one of us had to go.

"Sigfrid's life was wrecked . . ." The words still rang in my ears, and it was I who had spoken them. I understood now what I had done.

"How could you say such a thing?" demanded Mother. "It wasn't Father's fault that . . ."

No one in the kitchen ate any more. My little sister Linnea was crying. Jenny said, "We needn't carry on like idiots 'cause Father's lost his temper. He's done that often enough before."

He would soon come back, she thought; and so did Mother.

We waited. An hour passed; two hours. But Father did not return.

It was dark outside; night had come. Father couldn't be doing any outdoor work. What was he taking so long over? Where had he gone? We began to get uneasy.

204

And it was Mother who said, "You don't think he'd do anything to himself . . ."

Mother, Jenny and I lit the stable lantern and went out to look for Father. The April evening was chilly; it had snowed during the day, and now it was frosty and the snow crunched under our feet. In such cold as this Father must have gone into one of the buildings.

We looked in the cow shed, the barn, the hayloft. He was nowhere to be seen.

"Do anything to himself . . ." Coming from Mother, that meant only one thing.

If Father had done this thing—then there was no point in my sending back the ticket to America. Yet that was what I thought of doing. I didn't know my father; I had never dreamed that he would react like this when I said "In my pocket I've got . . ."

Mother knew him better than I did. She knew what he might do. And there was one way: I had heard of local people who had done it.

I went into the stable and looked. The ox reins were hanging in their usual place. I searched for the ropes that were usually to be found in the cow shed and the barn, and counted them, but I didn't know if they were all there, and I didn't want to ask Mother about it.

We went on looking and flashing the lantern here and there. We looked into the well, but we could see only water down there.

It was an evening of dread. Mother and Jenny began to get cold, and I persuaded them to go back to the house. I went on searching along the cattle track and in the sheep paddock. I stopped and shone the light onto the big juniper bushes that grew on the slope there, and thought how the biggest and handsomest of these were cut down at a funeral.

Now and then I called, "Father, Father!" There was no answer. I searched the copse too, but in vain. But when on my way back to the house I passed the potato cellar, I heard sounds from inside it. It sounded like muffled growling, and I wondered whether the cat had been shut up in there when we removed the potatoes that day. I opened the door and shone the lantern into the darkness.

In the light from it I saw my father. He was sitting on a basket of seed potatoes in the murk of the cellar, mumbling to himself, and as I opened the door I caught one word. He repeated it: "Alone . . . alone . . ."

I went in; I told him I'd been hasty, and was sorry for what I'd said. I asked him to forgive me.

He answered, "I been thinking all evening. I've changed my mind. All the same to me whether you go or stay."

"What—?"

"If you stay you'll still be gone. 'Cause I've lost you anyway. You go!"

✣

I was later the father of two sons myself, and have known the day when I found myself in my father's place, with my sons Albert and Andrew in mine.

Esther and I had different ideas as to how we should live our life together, but about the bringing up of our boys we were always in agreement: there was to be no corporal punishment. We did not believe that physical pain would help them, or that we would be doing them good by hurting them. I would have degraded myself in their eyes if I had used my superior strength as an argument against them: "Are you so weak that you

206

must resort to force?" My own father beat me in good faith, according to the fourth commandment; he beat me at God's express orders, to make me keep His laws. But I who did not believe in God would have had no such excuse for striking my children.

I did not want them to obey me from fear; yet I did try to teach them obedience. I wanted to teach them how to live, and I told them what to do and what not to do. I had lived thirty years longer than they had; I was experienced, I knew better than they. I was convinced that they would be helped by my advice, and I was persistent: they must follow it.

But they rejected the experience that I tried to impose upon them: they had nothing to learn from me, because they didn't want to live as I had lived.

I heard this twice, once from Albert and the second time from Andrew: "It's no good, Dad—I'm not going to obey you. After all, I know—you feel you've been a failure. Don't try to spoil my life too. What's happened to you won't happen to me."

So I got back what I had said to my own father. In different words and a different language, but it was the same thing—the same refusal to obey and the same admonition: Thou shall not ruin thy son's life!

When I recovered myself, I had no answer to make. Albert and Andrew needed me while they were small; as they grew up they slipped away from me, and after my divorce from their mother they were gone. They have been mature men for a long time now. They don't need me, and have made this very plain. But I need them. I feel a desperate need of my children.

My father sat one evening in our dark potato cellar murmuring, *"Alone . . ."* I became a lone man in a hotel room.

"THERE IS NOT ANOTHER TOWN anywhere quite like PINE BEACH," stated an editorial in our local paper yesterday. "It is a place where adults can continue their spiritual and mental growth."

We are having a pleasantly warm October in Pine Beach this year, with moderate winds. The Pacific has behaved peacefully, and has had no further outbreaks. But the fog is more troublesome than it usually is during this month, especially in the mornings. It irritates my throat, and I feel the pressure of it over my chest.

World crises, however, are a normal occurrence at this time of year; last September and October the Russians exploded their doomsday bombs over Novaya Zemlya. This year the threat has moved westward. A word of four letters grows daily larger in the headlines: Cuba! *Cuba!* CUBA!

The word follows me wherever I go; I hear it in the hotel, in conversations in the street, from loudspeakers and television sets. I cannot escape it. The name of the sugar island off the East Coast blares like the trump of doom across the continent, and terrifies the people on the West Coast.

CUBA: DEADLY THREAT
TO AMERICA!

Twice a day I buy papers from Mrs. Boles. Her drugstore does a thriving trade these days; people stampede for newspapers. Every day she increases her order, but there are never enough copies. In all the twenty years she has had her store, she has never seen anything like this run on them.

Press, radio and television combine to keep up the scare. Our mass media create an apocalyptic mood: People buy copies of the apocalypse and make profits by speculating in their own destruction.

Yesterday a famous atomic physicist made a pronouncement on the radio: Our technical resources for annihilation have now become so vast that it would be possible to consider constructing a machine capable of destroying this planet in one mighty explosion; a single explosion could transform our earth into small particles and send them whirling about the universe. The speaker estimated that this doomsday apparatus could be built for about ten billion dollars.

It is not the sale of newspapers alone that rises so steeply at any threat of global destruction. Mrs. Boles is kept busy filling prescriptions for sleeping pills, mostly strong ones that can be obtained only through a doctor. With every world crisis she notices the same thing: The demand for sleeping pills keeps pace with the size of the letters in the headlines; the increasing number of prescriptions reflects people's fears.

The narcotics industry thrives on the apocalyptic mood.

I too have to buy my night's sleep from Mrs. Boles. I have suffered another defeat in my many years of struggle against the powders that carry poison to one's body. Recently my sleep was broken by the movement of my furniture in my room. My bed became an unsafe resting place. Now I no longer feel those seismic forces as an imminent danger. At any time the crust of the earth may stir again and wake me—in bed, or under the rubble. But this possibility has been driven from my mind by the threat aimed at human life over the whole surface of the earth.

❧

How has man managed to arrive at this age of terror?

I look for the answer in his history, going as far back as I can. Lately I read Professor Ralph W. Sullivan's great work on American prehistory: *Before Columbus*. One self-evident truth that I had never reflected upon is that our continent is no younger than the rest of the earth; the New World is as old as any other part. The known continent of America is not yet five hundred years old, but the unknown one is of vast antiquity. America existed before Columbus. What races inhabited our continent in the millennia before Christ?

Professor Sullivan bases his work on the most recent researches into natural history. Here I may learn all that he knows of the discoveries made during recent decades by biologists, archeologists, geologists and researchers in other fields. From them the historian draws his conclusions and creates for me a picture of the America that was the contemporary of Homer, Socrates, Caesar, Christ, Mohammed, Attila, Charlemagne, Dante and Michelangelo.

Before Columbus the inhabitants of this continent lived in dread of wild beasts, floods, earthquakes, hurricanes, eclipses, supernatural forces. And they lived as we do: in terror of one another. But there is a difference between them and us: They were ignorant of the powers that frightened them, but we know the

210

ones that frighten us—we know what they can do to us. We ourselves have produced them.

In a way *Before Columbus* is a great source of comfort to me. Even as a boy I wanted to know how people lived before my own time; nothing came of my boyish dreams of becoming a historian. For Albert Carlson the businessman, history became recreation after the day's work, reading for the hours left over from the office. And in contemplating Professor Sullivan's work on America's past, I know that I would never have had the energy for the task of becoming a scientific historian. This is the kind of book I would like to have written, but I could never have done it. I might perhaps have managed to be a mediocre history teacher in some small-town high school, but I could have made no career for myself in the field of history.

There is a betrayal that cannot be forgiven: the betrayal of the powers bestowed on me. Have I misused them? What have I done with my share of energy? I perceive clearly that I have wasted all too much of my time on unimportant things; I have sacrificed days and years on trivialities and futilities. Why I have done this is a question that no one can answer, a riddle none can solve.

But I am only one of countless people who have failed to achieve what they intended in life; and there remains only one lifeline to strive for: the strength needed to accept this fact.

My friend Jesus Jensen has disappeared.

For a whole week I have missed him at the Surf-San Pedro intersection during the rush hour. He is no longer at his post, transmuting his doctrine of love into action and striving to save lives. Where has he gone? What can have happened to him?

Guests at the Pacific say they have heard that Jesus Jensen himself was run over and killed by a car at the San Carlos-Ocean Avenue crossing. He had been careless and ignored the traffic regulations. Such an accident would seem likely—even natural—but the rumor is false. My inquiries at the police station show that no traffic accident has occurred in Pine Beach in recent weeks. The police too are wondering what has become of Jesus Jensen.

Cabrillo of MEXICAN FOOD declares that my compatriot is locked up in a lunatic asylum: that in the house he shares with his sister and brother-in-law he started a big fire in the dining room, that the fire was discovered and put out in time, and that his sister and brother-in-law had him taken to a mental hospital. So the lunatic has come to his right home at last, says the Mexican.

I have had no confirmation of this, and I do not believe it. Yesterday I went to the house at the end of Stanton Street where Jesus Jensen lived, and rang the doorbell. No one answered it. The house seems empty at present.

All I know for certain is what I can see for myself: Jesus Jensen has vanished from his post.

This morning I had a letter from Annie. My second divorced wife is a faithful correspondent. Today she has a piece of news about herself: she is getting a divorce, moving from San Francisco, and taking up her old teaching job at Carmel High School. I suspect she intends to marry again, for the fourth time, though she

212

gives no hint of this. Why is she divorcing her third husband? She writes nothing about that either.

When after three years Annie and I still failed to find sexual satisfaction with each other, we agreed to separate. But our friendship has endured throughout the years since then, and I always think of Annie with gladness.

But the letter I am expecting didn't come today either. My son Albert had his thirty-fifth birthday on the last day of July, and I wrote in good time to give him my best wishes. We are now far on in October, and I have still had no answer.

I don't know where Albert is just now. The only address I have is a year old. He often moves about and my letter may never have reached him. Nor do I know what kind of life he is leading. Is some woman sharing it? He has been married three times; his first marriage lasted six months, and his second two years, and I don't know whether his third still lasts.

But my younger son is still happily married to his first wife; he has two lovely children, a girl and a boy. Andrew has done very well in business and concentrates all his efforts on expanding his manufacturing firm. Albert, who has pursued quite different occupations—acting, singing, flying—regards his brother's life as pointless. He once said, "No man is successful unless he has tried everything and failed in everything." No doubt by this he meant to console his father.

Albert inherited my passion for fishing. On our fishing trips to the waters round Iron Creek we had good times together. Andrew preferred to stay at home, but Albert was always eager to accompany me with rod and tackle to the beautiful lakes of Michigan and their leafy shores. Yet how many times were our trips postponed? How many times did my work interfere? I would promise my boy that we would go to this or that lake together—and then business matters arose, meetings, appointments with customers, sales to be closed at once, houses to be valued, rented, renovated, enlarged, sold. Many of our fishing trips never came off—because of business.

When he grew up and I tried to draw closer to him, he said, "When I needed you, Dad, you never had time for me. Now you're too late. Now I'll look after myself."

Five years ago Albert began training as an airplane pilot. When I last heard from him he had got a job with Pan American and was to start on the Tokyo route.

Mrs. Jeffers is back from her vacation in Mexico, and she has just called on me at my hotel with her promised surprise: the offer of a job in her real-estate office.

She has five employees there already, all women. But her business is expanding, there is more office work and consequently a larger staff is needed. She wants someone to deal chiefly with the bookkeeping; and I am an old hand who was in the business for many years. Mrs. Jeffers is convinced that she could find no one better suited than myself. She knows I am worth a higher salary than she can offer—but she offers me $500 a month.

She is obviously afraid that I shall say no at once. I don't. I would have, a month ago. But a great deal has happened to me since then, and I know now that the winding up of my affairs was just one more luckless attempt at escape. It may be my last.

I can stay on at the Pacific for one more month at most. After that my body will continue to need its daily food and a room with a bed in it at night. $500 a month, and I need $450 to stay on here. It would be enough.

I ask Mrs. Jeffers for time to think it over. I refer to the world crisis—*Cuba*. Just at the moment I feel as if we were on the eve of the Last Day; therefore I am disinclined to make any decision regarding the future. I beg her to understand this.

Mrs. Jeffers does not believe in an imminent nuclear war and the resulting destruction of the world. And in any event: business as usual. But she will wait for my answer before offering the job to anyone else.

Last night I took two sleeping pills, but woke at 1 A.M. Tonight I shall take three. I will remain in the depths of sleep while the other hemisphere turns toward the sun, and darkness is still with us here; for my persecutor keeps coming back and back and back. But at night I must drive it away from me—this thing confronting me: this *before*. In the daytime I am helped by my journeying through the past; and some part of that road remains.

I WAS BORN IN SWEDEN and emigrated to the United States at the age of twenty-two and have resided here for over forty years.

One evening in May, 1920, I boarded the express at the railway station near my home. My sister Jenny saw me off; Father and Mother refused to come. Jenny's cheerfulness never flagged, and when we said goodbye she joked about my journey. She wanted to say to me what the farmer said to his son when the boy left his home for the first time, to go out into the world: "May the Lord be with you as far as the gate. After that you just follow the main road."

My sister wished me the best of luck. I had become an emigrant.

After fifteen years in the United States I paid my first visit to my home district. By then Karlsson's home son Albert had been transformed into Mr. Albert Carlson, manager of Andrew W. Johnson's real-estate office in Iron Creek, Michigan, U.S.A., and husband of the proprietor's daughter and only child. I was a married man and the father of a family. Up to that time I had done well in the business, and my father-in-law, who had retired from it, was more than satisfied with me. From the financial point of view I had been very successful. My father realized this. He thought I had done right to seek my fortune abroad and that it was he who

216

had been wrong in trying to stop me from emigrating.

He never knew that I came home that time to see if I could possibly return to Sweden for good.

I had left my own country, yet even after fifteen years I did not feel at home in America—and knew by then that I never would. I had a larger income than I could spend, yet the work that brought it to me was utterly uncongenial. I had married one of the most beautiful women of Iron Creek, but we had ceased to love each other ten years before. I had two boys, but the office, business, and business trips stole so many hours of the twenty-four that I seldom had any time to give them. I had a big, modernly equipped house in Iron Creek, a summer place by a beautiful forest lake in northern Michigan, and a fashionable apartment in Chicago. But none of these dwellings ever became a home.

It was in this land of opportunity that I was to earn enough money to be free. I had earned that money— and felt like a prisoner in America. I was fenced round by obligations and duties; I was a father; I had a wife and children; when my father-in-law retired I had taken over the business; I had attained a certain position in the town and was bound by other people's claims on me, and by values that were not my own. I wanted to move from Iron Creek, but Esther would never leave her home town. I was imprisoned in Andrew W. Johnson's real-estate office: I had escaped from one jail to another.

My father must never know that his son had attempted flight: Could I be free if I came back? Where *did* I belong, after all? During my first visit to my home parish I realized that the lot of the emigrant was forever mine.

I was already a stranger—a Swedish-American who had just dropped by. I was changed, the people I knew were changed. I met old friends and schoolmates, but we had nothing to say to each other. Fifteen years of experiences in different countries separated us, as the Atlantic separates the continents. We tried gropingly to renew contact: "How's it going? How have things been? What are you doing now? Are you married? Any children? How long are you staying?"

I did not lie in answer to the questions they put to me, yet I wasn't truthful either. Vanity prevented this. The people who asked thought I had done well for myself in America: I had succeeded in life. Many of my old friends and companions were envious: Their resentment was plain to see, and it repelled me. Why hadn't they done what I had done?

I might have told them who it was that they were envying: an emigrant who had never found what he sought and who wanted to come back. But I would not afford them the pleasure of exchanging envy for glee.

My home parish was no longer home to me. But where *did* I belong? Nowhere?

My first visit to Sweden was a disappointment. But last summer when I paid my third and last, I had resigned myself to my lot. I came then from the land of orange trees, where fruit growing had brought me greater satisfaction than anything else I had done. I had owned a beautiful grove—a large area full of the trees that bore the golden fruit. I had delighted in the sight of my orange trees in bloom; I had followed the transition of blossom to fruit, and fruit to ripeness. I had harvested the crop that my trees had yielded me; I had offered it to people and felt that I was doing good

218

and useful work. And the sight of my last crop, stolen from me by frost, hit me mortally. Snow had covered my plantation, and through the snow gleamed the golden-yellow peel of its oranges.

Yet the cool juice of the golden fruit—the drink of morning—is not to be compared with another drink that I have tasted: the juniper beer that my mother made.

The juniper bush is my childhood's tree; the juniper berry brought the savor of copse and meadow to my mouth; nothing can compare with that drink. It is brewed from the fruit of that odd man out—that rugged, stubborn growth that is not to be uprooted, or cowed, or tamed. The juniper bush in the enclosures of my home place has been as near to me as a kinsman.

Last summer we met again for the last time. I flung my arms round the juniper bush on the slope; it met me with its sharp spikes and tore smarting wounds in my hands. The one that stayed behind, the steadfast, answered me, the renegade, "No!"

I had been away too long. The only one in my home country I wanted to feel a kinship with no longer wanted to know me; my only surviving relative had turned me away.

And I had known it for a long time: it was too late.

Mr. Albert Carlson, you old Swedish-American, who are now aware that your life is almost over, you have known this for many years: Man must have a root in the world; he must belong somewhere. He cannot abandon the land where he was born and adopt another country as his birthplace. Prattle about old and new mother countries is prattle only, and a lie. Either I have a country of my own, or I have not. Mother country is singular, never plural.

The country you knew as child and young man was the country you left. That was your fate; you could never find another homeland. Yet if you had obeyed your parents and stayed in your own village, your own country, you would have fretted your life away at having wasted it. You would have said, "This isn't what I wanted." For you are so fashioned that you cannot belong to anyone or anything. Therefore: Seek no peace outside *yourself!* You were born with a flaw in you, a creature never to feel at home anywhere on the earth. You wander hither and thither—yet you can be as out of place in Iron Creek as in your home parish of Sjöhult, as dissatisfied here in America as in any country on any other continent. How could you be otherwise, since you cannot even belong to anyone or anything, or feel any sense of belonging?

If you had believed in God or a Creator, you could have blamed Him. Now never in all eternity will you find anyone to blame. But now it is time to reconcile the warring factions within yourself, if you desire peace of mind while you still live.

Be comforted! Take this consolation: that you have used your capacities as best you could. You could do no better—you lacked the strength. What now? Do the only thing that still remains: Accept the emigrant and be reconciled with him. Forgive him for living under the delusion that any physical journeyings could help him here on earth!

220

WHEN I CAME TO AMERICA my recollection of Sigfrid altered. I often thought of my dead brother, but the remembrance of him did not hurt me as before. And at last I ceased to wonder how it was that he contracted his mortal illness.

I could have found out all about it while I was at home if I had addressed my questions to one particular person. But I shunned that person. Yet through him the truth was to reach me at last.

It happened long after I emigrated, during my first return home, when Sigfrid had been dead more than twenty years.

I visited Father and Mother in their little newly built home. They had sold the farm the year before, but kept a patch of ground where they built a house for their old age. It contained two rooms on the ground floor and one above; I slept upstairs.

One Sunday morning Father and Mother went to church and I stayed alone in the house. I had just got up and was going to make some coffee in the kitchen when there was a knock at the outer door. I went and opened it, to find a middle-aged man standing at the top of the steps. He was dressed like a gentleman, to use the local expression, and I took him to be a stranger to the district. Yet in his speech I detected some tinge of the local dialect.

"Don't you know me?"

I hesitated. His face reminded me of someone from my childhood: a younger man, with thinner cheeks and sharper chin, a man with a more slender body, someone whom I had seen in quite different clothes.

"I'm Artur Nyström. Remember me, Albert?"

"Yes—yes, of course I do. Are you Artur? Why, we're cousins."

"That's right. We're cousins."

"Sorry! Come in."

It was "my Artur." I explained why I hadn't recognized him at once—it was his clothes. He was in civvies, and I remembered him in uniform. I had last seen him dressed as a sergeant.

"Well, I'm a civilian now. Good many years since we've seen each other," Artur added as we went in and sat down.

Girls' Delight was still a handsome enough fellow, though with a bit of a potbelly. He had retired from the army some years before. Sweden's defense forces were scrapped ten years ago, he told me, and there was no future for a soldier. But he had a good job as manager of an estate in Östergötland. He was just taking a flying visit home to see his old parents, and had heard that I was back from America for the same reason. He wanted to meet me, as we happened to be in the old home district at the same time. We were relatives, after all, and it had been a long time. . . .

Artur Nyström was more than ten years older than I; he had been a grown man when I was still a child, so although we had seen each other often enough, we hardly knew each other, and our conversation was somewhat labored, as between two strangers.

I mentioned Sigfrid.

"Yes, I served in the same regiment as him."

"I remember. You were an N.C.O."

It was then I began to understand that Artur had come to see me for a particular reason: "Don't suppose you ever knew just what happened—that nasty business with your brother?"

"Not from him. We gathered he was hurt on maneuvers."

"He told me all about it when he was in the hospital. I had to promise him to keep my mouth shut. But it's a long time since he died, so there's no harm in telling you all about it now—telling you what he did."

"What he did?"

Even before he said this—from the tone in which he spoke of my dead brother—I knew I was going to hear something quite different from what I had imagined and expected: something he was reluctant to talk about—for *Sigfrid's* sake.

Artur couldn't look me in the face when he told me; he stared down the road. "Your brother took himself off."

A dialect phrase I had had time to forget: *took himself off?*

"Nearly got jailed for it."

I was speechless. Jailed!

And the ex-sergeant in Sigfrid's regiment went on to tell me: Sigfrid and he had no contact with each other, since the Volunteer Training School and his own company were separate units. Moreover, there was the gulf between private soldiers and N.C.O.s, though that didn't prevent them mixing when off duty; Artur himself paid no attention to the restriction. He and my brother were cousins; they were born in the same district and had much in common to talk about. From the

223

moment Sigfrid joined up at the new year he had tried to show him the ropes. He could see that the newcomer was unhappy under the pressure and discipline of military service, but so were most recruits. It was just that they weren't used to it. They got over it in time.

A few times Artur had had coffee with Sigfrid at Bethany, the Baptist Soldiers' Home just outside the barracks area, although this place was really only for private soldiers. There was a reading and writing room in Bethany, where Sigfrid liked to go, and where he sat when off duty. Of his conduct on duty there had been nothing but good reports. He had no reports against him; never received the slightest punishment; he behaved well in the school. Moreover he was big and strong and well able to carry out the exacting tasks of the volunteer recruits.

But one day in March Artur got wind of a horrible story in the N.C.O.s' mess: One of the members of the school, while on a night march, had committed a very serious breach of army regulations. During this march he had lain down, merely saying that he would go no farther: he had refused to obey orders. He was a straggler. There was nothing the matter with him. But later he was sick, and was now in the regimental hospital. The volunteer's name was Karlsson.

Artur could not believe that it was Sigfrid; there were several volunteers named Karlsson. But he went at once to the hospital to make sure—and what he hadn't been able to believe was true.

Sigfrid had been admitted to the hospital with a severe chill and an inflammation of the throat so bad as to lead to an infection of the kidneys. There was blood in his urine and he ran a high fever.

Having visited the patient several times, Artur discovered what Sigfrid had done—on condition he told nobody else, lest it should leak back home.

He hadn't been in the service for three days before he knew that he could never stand three years of it. At home they had advised him to enlist, and he had signed the paper; but for that he blamed no one but himself. He didn't want to handle weapons; he never had wanted to. But in a couple of years he would have been forced to do his military service anyway, so he had thought he might just as well volunteer and get the good free schooling that was offered. He would just have to sweat out the rifle practice, he thought.

Only he couldn't stand the rifle range. The cardboard dummies came alive when he shot at them—they became people who cried out to him not to aim, not to fire. It seemed to him that when he hit the dummies he was killing people. And after bayonet practice he had vomited several times—he had puked like a cat.

This had gone on for over two months, and he realized that he would never get through three years of it. He was forced to get out—he couldn't help it, he said. He would work it so as to be dishonorably discharged. It could be done if he committed a grave breach of army regulations: he would refuse to obey an order. After that they could do what they liked with him.

His platoon was detailed for a night march—and the night was a cold one. When they had been marching along the high road for about an hour, he told the N.C.O. in front of him, "This is where I leave the service." He then fell out and lay down by the roadside, in a ditch, with full equipment: rifle, pack, the lot. The platoon officer blew his top and threatened him with a court-martial if he didn't obey orders and get up again. He lay where he was and the platoon marched on.

225

He had marched himself hot and sweaty, but soon he got cold. (The temperature was close to 5° that night.) He got up and began walking again to get some warmth into himself. But he didn't know the roads in those parts; he got lost and wandered about for the rest of the night and half the next day before he found his way back to the barracks. Exhausted, he fell into bed in his quarters. That night he shivered as if in an ague, and they took him to the hospital.

He had never thought, said Sigfrid, how dangerous it might be to lie down in the snow, wet with sweat, in such cold. But now he knew: he would never be well again.

What he had done was quite beyond Artur's comprehension, as Artur himself told Sigfrid. There would have to be a court-martial, and his refusal to obey the orders of his superior might result in two years' imprisonment or hard labor. So he wouldn't be free. On the contrary, he would be confined in the fortress.

But couldn't he be discharged from the regiment after committing a crime like this? Sigfrid had asked Artur. That was all he wanted. And whatever they might do with him now, he didn't care.

He was kept in the regimental hospital until May; by then he was well enough to get up. He was discharged and sent home.

There was never any court-martial; the case was dismissed. They couldn't put a sick man in prison. The commandant of the Volunteer Training School wanted to bury that man's gross breach of discipline in oblivion, as it would damage the school's reputation, he told Artur, who had also spoken to the Medical Officer about him. The chill had brought on a chronic disease: nephritis. The doctor had not held out hope of any cure, but merely told the patient that if he got plenty of rest and was careful with his diet, he might live for a long time.

But he lived only a couple of months after his discharge. Perhaps he didn't look after himself properly when he got home, or perhaps there was some complication—that was something I would know better than he, Artur Nyström ended.

I had listened to my cousin without interrupting him once.

Only now did I know through and through the man he spoke of—only now did I know the man that Sigfrid was.

We were both silent for a while.

Then my visitor resumed. "I wanted to tell you this. Could have told you before, but you were away."

"I'm grateful."

"Your father asked me about it once, and I said I didn't know."

"I've always wondered what happened to my brother."

"Well, at least he escaped prison. And I don't want to blacken his memory."

"No, I realize that."

"He was so afraid of his family's knowing. Are you going to say anything to your mother and father?"

"No, I'm not."

"Best they shouldn't know that their son brought it all on himself. He might have ended up in the fortress."

After all that "my Artur" had said, I had hardly anything to say to him. He talked of my brother as of a criminal who had dodged his punishment.

He made it even harder for me by asking, "Have

227

✿✿✿✿

As SOON AS I GET OUT OF BED in the morning I tear yesterday's page from the calendar. October—we're in the
third week of the month and will soon enter the fourth
and last. Outside my room the life of town and ocean
continues—the life that will vanish and the life that
will go on.

Down on Surf I see Mrs. Jeffers going to work,
sturdy and assured. At nine o'clock on the dot she is in
her office, where at once the telephone starts ringing. A
job is waiting for me there; it would be a short and
easy way to work, half a minute from my hotel. Seven
hours a day, five days a week, an hour off for lunch,
Saturdays free, $500 a month—a generous offer to a
tired old bookkeeper of sixty-four, an unsuccessful
runaway.

Mrs. Jeffers awaits my answer. Yet soon something
may happen to release me from my promise to answer:
Cuba. From the skies may fall the stuff of destruction
—at any moment. It has already begun—it has been
going on for a long time. Mankind is beginning to fear
its food, its drink, the baby's milk—that most innocent
of drinks.

I open my east window and look up at the clouds
that float in the clear light of morning. Our Father is
no longer in heaven. Christ will not come upon the

230

clouds of heaven to search out our hearts and judge the living and the dead. But from those clouds will fall a rain that will seep into our blood. Christ has no need to descend to us with his judgment: We can get it for ourselves.

But I shall search my own heart no longer. I neither condemn nor acquit Mr. Albert Carlson; I shall let him be what he is, since I can do nothing about him. But where did I get that designation "bookkeeper" for him?

It was part of one of the decisive events of my life.

Esther and I had had a tremendous row; our marriage had been unhappy for a long time, and the subject of divorce cropped up about once a week in our conversation. But now I had spoken from the very depths of my soul: of my dislike of Andrew W. Johnson's real-estate office, of my boredom with Iron Creek and everything connected with my wife's home town. I wanted to give up my work, move out and start a whole new life. Every day spent in my father-in-law's business increased my self-contempt.

It was then that Esther said, "Oh, you little *bookkeeper!*"

She knew where to hurt me. I had begun as her father's accountant and had kept the firm's books for many years. And she said to me, "You're the most ungrateful person I've ever met. It was my father who gave you your chance when he took you on—he helped you, and it's through him and your marriage to me that you've got where you are. You owe everything to my father and me!"

This was not strictly true; I owed it to my own effort and energy. Yet there was enough truth in her words to make them more than I could take.

The blood rushed to my brain, and I went mad. I had never lost control with my sons, but with my wife I did. I had never struck my children, but I struck their mother.

I hit Esther in the face—her mouth. Hard. "You little *bookkeeper!*" I hit the mouth that spoke those words. Without my thinking, my hand flew out to silence that mouth—to stifle it.

Her blow had gone home; so did mine. Blood flowed from the corners of my wife's mouth; it ran down her chin, streaking her delicate white skin with red.

I had drawn blood from the woman with whom, as a mature man, I had fallen hopelessly in love—the only woman whom in my adult life I ever loved.

Esther took the blow in silence. She uttered not a sound. Her lips bled and quivered, but she said nothing; she merely looked at me, without astonishment or shock. She just calmly looked.

In a few moments I was myself again—or what I hoped was myself. I could not think what had come over me. I begged forgiveness; could she forgive me?

Esther took out a handkerchief and started wiping the red streaks of blood from her chin: "You don't have to apologize. You can't help being what you are —and neither can I."

She kept her eyes on me steadily—not in hatred or bitterness. There was no wrath in her eyes; she was not angry. If there had been rage or hatred in her face, I could have stood it. But the look in my wife's eyes was contemptuous, superior, pitying—therefore unendurable to me.

I had degraded and humiliated myself, and nothing further needed to be said between us. The battle between us was over. She had won. I revealed myself as

232

the weaker one, the inferior of the two. Tomorrow, maybe, she would take back the words that had driven me out of my mind; for I knew she could never feel completely indifferent about me or dismiss me as a creature worthy of scorn and pity. But from my position as her husband I had now to be released.

On the day following this incident Esther and I filed for a divorce.

I believed I had freed myself. Many years passed before I acquired the certainty that freedom was to be won only within myself.

I have had news of Jesus Jensen. This evening he was announced on the radio as a missing person. He had left his home in Pine Beach. There followed a detailed description of his appearance and dress—both well known to every inhabitant of our town. The missing man had told several people that he intended to go to Death Valley. Any information was to be communicated to his sister Mrs. Jenson-Harrington, Harrington House, Stanton Street, or to the Pine Beach Police Department.

My compatriot the Dane has walked forth into the California desert, where at this time of year the air temperature may rise to 122°. I know his purpose: He has gone to prospect for the place where the bodies of car-murdered people are to be collected. He is in the desert to find the place where the Great Warning is to be erected, where there will be built a pyramid of corpses—a monument of lifeless bodies to be increased annually by 40,000, to rise nearer to heaven every year. In ten years' time it will comprise almost half a million. And from the top of this pyramid of dead a warning shout will go out to the living: Look at us! Stop driving!

Listening to the announcement, I think of a precursor of Christ: John the Baptist, who lived in the desert on locusts and wild honey. Jesus Jensen is a heathen, and in the deserts of California, so far as I know, there are no locusts or wild honey or any other edible thing. And at this time of year all rivers, creeks and springs are dry; there is no drinking water in the Valley of Death.

Jesus Jensen stands no longer at the Surf-San Pedro intersection, and I have a strong feeling that no one in Pine Beach will ever see him again.

But I hear him: "I shall succeed. I've staked my life on the project."

One man set forth alone into the great desert; another fell out of the ranks and lay down in a snowdrift in a wayside ditch.

❦

I am waiting for a letter that didn't come in today's mail. It will come tomorrow.

Another page is torn off. Today we have had the decisive, unequivocal pronouncement from the President of the United States:

"It shall be the policy of this nation to regard any nuclear missile launched from Cuba against any nation in the Western Hemisphere as an attack by the Soviet Union on the United States, requiring a full retaliatory response upon the Soviet Union."

Now everybody is waiting—just waiting.

Today it is closer to me than ever: I feel as if it were imminent, this *before*—my own *before*. And I turn to those who have already been through it; I ask how they managed and how they felt. I seek their strength, reach out for their helping hands, grope for some support from their example. I want to know what it was like—and how they *could*.

I once sat by a sickbed in a little house in a village, situated in another part of the globe. I sit there again, with my father.

He has been dead these thirteen years—but it is from him I seek help: *How did you manage it, Father?*

✿✿✿✿

MY FATHER LIVED to be eighty-four. In all his life he spent only three weeks in bed, and those weeks were his last. That was in the summer of 1949. I heard he was seriously ill, and for the first time I went to Sweden by air; when I arrived he had a week left.

As soon as I had greeted the sick man in his bed, he said, "This is the last of me. Might as well say so at once."

I tried to express the doubt I did not feel, but he interrupted me: "I'll soon be gone. So long as you know it, we don't have to say more about it."

I had confirmation of this from the local doctor who had attended Father: There was no doubt of the diagnosis. Liver—a growth, probably cancer. The patient could be admitted to a hospital, but it would do no good, and he wanted to stay at home and be cared for by his daughter; my sister Jenny had lived with Father since Mother's death. There was no question of a long illness, the doctor said. For cancer patients of that age the period of suffering was short. He had done all that remained to be done in this case: he had prescribed pain-killing drugs.

The doctor thought he had given me a report on my father that might satisfy me.

In Father's bed I saw an altered, diminished human

face and an emaciated, shriveled body. The sick man could take hardly any food; almost all he ate came up again, mourned Jenny. Father, who had always been such a hearty eater—she had never seen anyone chew and swallow with such gusto.

I told Father that he must try to eat.

"What's the use when the body doesn't want to go on any longer?"

Father's body had deserted him; it refused to be fed and kept going; it had made up its mind.

I sat down by his bed, and he raised his head from the pillow: he would have liked to stay in the world a few more years, but it was his turn now to go, and there was nothing to be done about that. No good moaning. What was the use of fighting something we all had to go through? "I've lived enough anyhow. I'm not grumbling."

I listened in silence; I had no answer.

Father and I had shared about fifty years of time on this earth, yet we were as good as strangers to each other. We never understood each other when we lived under the same roof, and now we had been at opposite ends of the earth for a long time. During my childhood he was the one who commanded, I the one who obeyed. When I grew older and began disputing his paternal rights over me, our battles began. But when I came back on my first visit after emigrating, we were reconciled; bygones should be bygones. Never after that, by letter or in any other way, had we touched upon old matters.

Now Father lay on his deathbed and I had come to see him.

"We won't talk about dying any more," said Father. "Not when there's no getting out of it."

From the beginning he had dismissed the subject of his imminent death. After that all other topics lost content. What was there to talk of? What more was there for us to say to each other?

Father got breathless when he talked. I sat silent in a basket chair by his bed while he recovered his breath.

He resumed: "You staying for the funeral?"

"Surely you don't have to ask me that, Father."

"I just thought—you're always in such a hurry, boy."

The term "boy" addressed to a man of fifty sounded so natural coming from my father that I never noticed it. But his question as to whether I meant to stay for his burial revealed the gulf between us.

"You were in such a hurry last time."

"But this time I came home because . . . because I'd heard—" I broke off.

"People are in such a terrible hurry these days—as if they were trying to snatch butter out of the fire. All so afraid they won't be in time. In time for what?"

I saw Father as he was in my childhood, running from one job to another. He never gave himself time to walk; he always moved at a jog trot.

I reminded him of this: Who had been afraid of not getting things done in time if not himself?

"True enough, boy," said Father. "Could've hurried a little less myself, and still been in time for my deathbed."

He closed his eyes and talked more slowly and softly. "It's all gone by so quick—in a flash, like. It was life itself that speeded up. I didn't need to hurry."

I had arrived late in the evening. My sister interrupted my first talk with Father; she was going to give him his pain-killer now, and after that he usually fell asleep. So far she hadn't had to sit up with him all night, but she always got up once or twice to have a look at him. He had attacks of vomiting.

Jenny and I were to take turns at sitting up, if necessary. I said good night to Father and went up to the little room on the upper floor where I was to sleep.

Father and I talked together for a few hours every day; and during that last week of his life I got to know him better than in all the years that had gone before.

❧

When I came down to Father next morning he seemed rested. I saw at once that he had urgent things on his mind.

He said, "Want to talk about the funeral."

"You don't have to worry about that, Father."

"But I wanted to tell you how I'd like it done."

"It'll be all just as you say."

"Yes. Will you see to it?"

"You can trust me." His wishes should be fulfilled as far as possible.

"Six fellers to carry the coffin," said Father.

"Yes."

"We'll have the old 'uns—if there's enough of 'em."

I knew the old funeral customs of my district: Young people were carried to the grave by the young, old by the old. I myself had helped to carry people of my own age.

"Will you ask the six fellers?"

"Yes, of course. I'd better write down their names." I didn't trust my memory, so I found pen and paper.

"I was thinking out the six last night."

He half sat up in bed. The first man was Aron

Johan, who had been his nearest neighbor for many years; he was over eighty, but spry and fit, and he could certainly manage his share of the coffin. Only that spring Father had helped to carry Johan's cousin's coffin, and he had been as light on his feet as a boy. The next one should be Frans of Övergård. He was delicate and had backache, although only seventy-five, but he could certainly give a hand. The coffin wouldn't be all that heavy. As third and fourth men he thought of Emil Eliasson and his son. Emil and Father had been on bad terms for many years, having fallen out over a boundary, but after they had both left their farms and begun to decline, they made it up again. Emil was a year older than Father and not very active now, but he would not refuse. The bearers wouldn't need much strength anyhow, for there wouldn't be much left of him in the end.

Father coughed and gasped for breath. He was shrinking away even while he was alive; most was being taken from him beforehand, so there wouldn't be much left for the coffin. It was just as well.

Three pairs of bearers, six men, were needed. There were not enough old men, and we should have to have two more from a younger generation. Father chose a couple of the new farmers whom he knew to be decent fellows. He wanted good honest folk to carry him to the grave.

I wrote down the six names and read them out to him.

He seemed pleased: "They'll do fine. Good fellers, all of them."

"I'll have a word with them."

"I've spoken to Aron Johan myself. He's promised to say a few words first."

"First? When?"

"In the morning before they start for church, of course. By the coffin, I mean."

Aron Johan, that faithful old neighbor, would have said a few words even if he hadn't been asked, so he had told Father. He had always been a helpful man. And there should be a few words of praise spoken when a person passed on, however he had lived and behaved and however many enemies he may have had.

"I don't think you'll be leaving any enemies behind you, Father."

The sunken face of the sick man twitched; he was in pain.

"You must rest for a while."

"May be. But first will you get the ration book out of the bureau?"

"What for?"

"I'll write my name in it. You must buy some for me."

I remembered now; it was a little book of coupons for buying spirits, such as was used at that time in Sweden.

"Get the whole allowance for the month."

"I'll see to it."

"They must have a brandy in their coffee in the morning, before they go to church."

With Jenny's help I found the book in one of the drawers of the bureau and gave it to him.

"Here are two liters left for the month. Buy one liter of brandy and the other of *brännvin*."

"I will."

"One brandy each in the morning, and the rest when they come back in the afternoon."

241

The little book lay on the coverlet in front of Father. I handed him a pen and he sat up to sign his name. It was slow business; his hand shook and the letters straggled. Once or twice he rested his hand as if hesitating to finish, but he completed his signature at last.

"Badly written, o' course. But they passed it before."

"They'll pass it all right."

The letters were crooked, they climbed above the line and sank under it, but the name was in the right place on the form, clearly readable: *Ernst Gottfrid Karlsson*.

After signing, Father settled himself back in bed again and his breathing was labored.

"Will you give me some o' them strong drops, boy?"

I gave him a spoonful of the analgesic medicine. He clasped his hands on his chest and closed his eyes.

I left him alone, for he needed rest.

He had signed his name for the last time.

In the afternoon he had a severe attack of vomiting. When he recovered from it he wanted to talk to me. "I doze off now and then, but sit with me anyway."

"Yes, if you'd like me to."

"Been lying here thinking about the old days. I was strict with you when you were at home. You had to start work early."

"I think now it was good for me."

"You had to start the year we came to the farm," said Father. "You were only nine."

I remembered. I had to go with my flail to the threshing floor when I was nine. Long before daybreak I had to get up and go out to the granary. My flail was

242

small, but the important thing was to keep time with the others, as that helped in the threshing. Sometimes it had snowed the night before so that I couldn't get through the drifts, and then Father carried me on his back.

I told him I was all the better for his having taught me to work when I was young, and I was grateful to him. I had been strong enough, I could manage it, and for healthy children there was no better upbringing than physical work. Children who learned to do things won self-confidence early.

"You had to learn the same as my father taught me: to earn your keep as soon as you could."

"We were poor, as I well remember."

"Yes, we were poor. And our children got thrashed when they didn't obey. I beat you so's you'd obey."

"I remember."

"But you didn't—you went to America. Just as well. Best for you."

I was silent.

"I beat you too often, maybe."

"Don't think about that now."

Everything that had happened between us in the past must be forgiven and forgotten on both sides, I added. I had said some terrible things to him the evening my ticket to America came, and he had forgiven me—those things should be forgotten forever. He would never mention them again.

Father now thought he had beaten me too hard in my childhood.

I looked at the hands that lay still on the bedcover. They had hit me, boxed my ears, hurt me. They had been big, bony, hard hands—I had learned just how hard they were. Now they lay on the cover limp and slack, shriveled and powerless. I saw a pair of shrunken hands, with wrinkled skin over sharp knuckles, emaciated fingers—they were already like parts of a skeleton.

Father had had the heavy hands of the manual worker. Now they had done their job; now all that remained to them was the reward for what they had achieved.

"I lie here thinking sometimes. I wonder . . ." Father looked at me with narrowed little eyes, deeply sunk under his brow—the eyes of the old. "I think about Sigfrid. I oughtn't to have gone on at him to enlist."

"You thought it was the best thing for him."

"Yes; he was to get all he needed free, and pay, and free schooling. I meant it all for the best. And it turned out so badly. Whose fault was it?"

Whose indeed? Sigfrid didn't want to handle weapons, but joined up voluntarily. I had made up my mind to have nothing to do with money, and went into business. Sigfrid was an obedient son, but lived only nineteen years. I was a disobedient son and I had lived a long time.

I might have told my father about myself and my sons, about my failure with them and my inability to learn anything about them. Parents can give their children the means of staying alive—but how often can they help them to live? Father could never help me; was the fault his or mine?

The sick man turned on his side and heaved a long sigh: "It's all so long ago. Almost seems it never happened."

Father was very tired now. Jenny came in and said

I'd been talking to him too long. We didn't resume the conversation till next day.

As my father's life neared its end, I came to know him. When he was on his deathbed I came close to him. I felt a respect that was different from that of the boy, which was born of fear. Faced with the inevitable, he showed a courage that I would not have believed he possessed.

During a long life of work on the soil he had learned the cycle of growing, living things. He had watched close at hand the growth of the crops from green shoot to the ear, from ripening to reaping. He had sown his seed corn, had seen it spring up, turn from green to yellow and be threshed, and crushed at last between the millstones. He had seen animals born, grow up, be fattened and then led forth to slaughter. He had become at one with the cycle of nature that he had experienced all about him throughout his farming life. He had followed the process, accepted it. That was how things were, and they could be no different. One just had to put up with it. And he was a part of it; he too would disappear and become dust. It was so simple; one just had to make up one's mind to it.

Father was a Christian and a churchgoer, but I never saw him turn to the Christian faith on his deathbed. Perhaps he said his prayers silently to himself, but he expressed no need of the consolations of religion. And I don't think he was worried about what was to come—about any punishment or reward that might be awaiting him. He behaved like the old pagans who, believing in an inexorable destiny, waited for death without complaint or lamentation or moaning. What was to happen to him was predestined and could not be altered.

During his last days Father displayed a strength that I marveled at. He grew in stature on his deathbed.

※

The doctor came to see Father a couple more times. Father's attacks of vomiting became more frequent, but he slept the greater part of the night and also for much of the day; the medicine helped him to sleep, the doctor said.

One morning when I came down Jenny told me that he had talked confusedly in the night. Now his head was clear again, but he spoke now of one thing and now of another, and I could see that he was uneasy in his mind.

He said, "We were talking of friends and enemies. But I'm afraid I'm leaving an enemy behind."

"Who can that be?"

"My cousin."

"Corporal Nyström, do you mean?"

"I got no other cousin."

"Why aren't you friends with him?"

"It was when we lost Sigfrid. Couldn't put up with him after that. 'Cause he wasn't honest."

Bit by bit, with interruptions, I gathered the reason for the breach. Sometime after Sigfrid's death there had been a violent scene between Father and the corporal first class. He had accused Nyström of deceiving Sigfrid, of describing life in the regiment as a paradise. There was all the good schooling he was to have, the splendid future when he would be promoted and have authority over others. Most of that was lies, Father realized afterward, and he threw it in the corporal's face. Father told him that he had fooled and misled his son, and accused him straight out of having done it for the sake of the recruiting money.

"I called Nyström a grasping devil."

The corporal threatened to sue him for defamation of character; and thus the enmity between them had arisen. They had been enemies ever since, and when they met on the road they pretended not to see each other.

But Father now thought that he had been unfair to his cousin. Nyström couldn't be blamed for Sigfrid's death. It had been on his conscience for some time that he had wronged his cousin, and now he wanted to tell him so. He wanted to be reconciled with him.

Corporal Nyström was his only enemy, and now that Father was going, he wanted to leave no enemy behind him.

"Can you send for Nyström?" asked Father. "Ask him to come and see me?"

"I'll do it at once."

I went out to my sister Jenny in the kitchen: Did she know where ex-corporal Nyström lived now? He was Father's cousin and was probably about as old —over eighty. Perhaps he was in the parish old people's home?

Jenny looked at me in astonishment. "Nyström? You mean the old corporal?"

"That's the one. Father wants us to send for him."

"But Corporal Nyström's dead."

"You don't mean it!"

"Yes, he died about five years ago," said Jenny.

I stared at her. "But Father speaks of him as if he were alive."

"I was in church the Sunday they buried him," Jenny said, "so I ought to know."

"But then why does Father say—? "

She made a gesture of her hand to her head: "He gets muddled sometimes. He was like that last night."

Father had waked up in the night and asked to speak to Mother; he thought she was asleep in the same room. Jenny reminded him that Mother had been dead for years, but he paid no attention. He wanted her to wake Mother. He was obstinate: He had to talk to her—it was very important. And when Jenny failed to obey him, he called out to Mother himself. He called loudly several times during the night. Jenny was on the point of coming to wake me; but then the old man fell asleep again.

I went back to Father and sat down in the chair by his bed. "Corporal Nyström can't come. He died five years ago."

Father raised his head a little from the pillow and looked at me in amazement: "My cousin the corporal. Yes, he's dead. Didn't you know?"

"No—not until Jenny told me."

"Yes, well—you been away a long time. You can't know everything that goes on here, can you?"

Father had forgotten all that he had said a little while before, and forgotten the errand he had given me to do. But now he was clear in his head and speech and remembered the past clearly.

"Yes, my cousin's dead. I wasn't asked to the funeral. We weren't friends."

"Yes, you told me."

"But we'd begun to nod to each other again the last few years. And I sent a wreath."

"You might have made it up, then."

"Yes. A pity we didn't talk it over together. Neither of us wanted to speak first. But I bought him a fine wreath—you ought to've seen it."

Father pondered silently for a long time. Then he said, "Nyström's dead. So I'm not leaving an enemy behind me."

🌳

Father's fits of rambling came at shorter intervals now, and his clear-headed periods at longer ones. My sister Jenny and I took turns at sitting up with him at night. He was quiet and peaceful again now.

The end came upon us unexpectedly. One night I dozed off in the basket chair by his bed. I slept for only a short time, but when I woke I saw a change in his face—a new stillness. He had stopped breathing.

He was asleep when I dropped off, but he never slept through to an awakening; instead he reached the sleep without end. It did not seem as if Death and he had wrestled together; they had just met and were of one mind.

I only wish that I may be able to disappear as Father did, with the quiet naturalness of a withered leaf dropping from the branch and sinking gently and softly to the ground.

✟✟✟

ON THE SHORES of the Pacific Ocean, between town and sea, a man has his dwelling place. He lives between the changing and the changeless. He has had many houses during his long life, but never a home. He inhabits a temporal room where he fights an awareness that he cannot evade. It comes to him by day and by night; it is with him again in the morning. Awareness pursues a man who has never had roots.

But there is one safe refuge.

In the evenings I walk out along the seashore. It is October, a good month on this coast; the winds are mild, the temperature pleasant. It is October, 1962, and all seems well on this earth.

The sand dunes are deserted; I meet no one. The ocean lies windless and still, and darkness has deepened over the waters; shore and sea have crept under its mantle. Only the white rims of foam hiss far out there in the blackness. The expanse of water is hidden from my eyes, but my ears hear its surge and swell. I hear the sea as the rumble of an approaching express train in the distance—a train that never comes any nearer, that is always on the way but never arrives. Never silent, never stopping: a train without stations, without a terminus. I hear a train in eternal movement, going nowhere.

250

I walk along the Pacific shore, just above the high-water mark. I am alone on the dunes tonight. The sand sinks under my feet.

In the beginning there was water. And it is still the eve of the first day of Creation. The firmament is not yet made nor the waters divided; no living thing moves yet, neither in the depths of the sea nor on dry land. "The earth is without form and void, and darkness is upon the face of the deep."

There is a tremendous din overhead. From the air comes a powerful noise that splits the silence ruthlessly. It comes from high over the sea and is suddenly directly above me—a searing, agonizing din.

What is this above the water?

Aircraft passing overhead—big military aircraft high over the ocean, borne on motionless steel wings. Their noise cuts my eardrums like the points of knives. I cannot see them in the darkness, but in the daytime I have often watched them flying along the coast on their regular route.

This is *Air Alert,* the sky patrol out on its daily routine flight and filling the air above with its harsh voices. These planes carry the weapons of doomsday in their holds; loaded weapons are ready aboard them, nuclear weapons. They fly over me with annihilation and the End in their entrails. The horsemen of the Apocalypse ride their winged steeds in the sky.

It is the spirit of man flying above the waters.

They pass in a moment; a few seconds later the din of *Air Alert* has died away. The air is free once more from the sound of the horsemen of heaven. Silence returns; nothing has happened.

But in the distance I hear as before the train that never comes, the murmur of the waters before they

251

were divided. A symbol of change has flown by; changelessness remains.

In a dark sky that embraces the sea the stars are kindled. They will shine down on the earth when the light of day has gone. I hear the distant train continuing its journey; I see the lights of heaven still in the place where they were set. Man with his speeding hour of din and death has gone, but waters and stars remain. Still.

Peace sinks into my soul: your time too will soon be over. But nothing means anything, when even this that you hear and see tonight will one day have passed away. After that there is nothing of importance left for you. You are at the beginning and at the end. And for you there is neither beginning nor end. In that certainty you may be safe.

In this is your safety.

I continue my walk along the beach, moving with calm, slow steps over the dunes. Close behind me the sea water runs in and fills my footprints in the sand.

❦ About the Author ❦

Carl Artur Vilhelm Moberg was born of peasant stock in the parish of Algutsboda, province of Småland, Sweden. He worked as a forester and a farmhand before becoming a journalist and then an author. He has published twenty novels and twenty-five plays, and his books have been translated into eighteen languages.

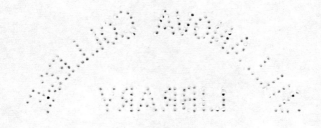